Maisey Yates is a *New York Times* bestselling author of more than thirty romance novels. She has a coffee habit she has no interest in kicking, and a slight Pinterest addiction. She lives with her husband and children in the Pacific Northwest. When Maisey isn't writing she can be found singing in the grocery store, shopping for shoes online and probably not doing dishes. Check out her website: maiseyyates.com.

Visit the Author Profile page at
millsandboon.co.uk for more titles.

This book is dedicated to the librarians.
I spent countless hours at libraries,
reading countless books.
Thank you for giving the joy of reading to everyone.

CHAPTER ONE

IT HAD BEEN a perfect night. So beautiful, the white Christmas lights strung across the facades of the buildings in Vail glittering on the snow all around them. Like the stars had dropped down from the sky to light their way.

Yes, the night had been perfect and Raphael even more so. But then, he always was.

Bailey couldn't quite believe it was real. Even after eight months with him, she couldn't believe it. He was like something out of a fairy tale, and she was a girl who never thought she'd have a happy ending.

But then she'd met him.

Of course, she only saw him every few months, when he flew into Colorado on business, and never for long enough.

She'd been guarded all of her adult life. So cautious when it came to men and dating. But with Raphael…that caution had never been there. She'd just given herself to him with no thought of self-protection, no thought of anything but how much she wanted him.

She was like a different woman with him. A woman in love.

It was always so frantic when he was there. Tonight

was no exception. They'd finished dinner, a walk through the town, then back to the hotel, where he'd consumed her.

There had been an edge to him tonight, an intensity. Not that she was complaining.

She stretched out on the sheets, curling her toes. She was still recovering. She giggled and rolled onto her side, looking toward the bathroom.

The door was closed, a sliver of light visible beneath it. She sighed heavily, waiting for him to come back to bed.

Waiting *impatiently*.

Tonight felt different. Significant and special.

She loved him so much. She ached with it. She'd never thought she could feel this way about someone. Never thought someone could feel this way about her.

She was ready for more. She was ready for everything.

The bathroom door opened, and her heart skipped a little. That made her smile. It was ridiculous how giddy she was over him. But then, she'd never let a man close enough to her to have this kind of intimacy.

In her waitressing job she got hit on by men all the time. She just wasn't…swayed by it. At all. She had been thoroughly disenchanted with men by the time she'd moved out of her mother's home at sixteen. She'd seen too much. Too much heartbreak. Too much screaming.

Bailey had decided to make her own life, her own future. She'd made it to twenty-one a virgin because she'd been so determined to wait until it was right, until she was ready.

And then she'd met Raphael. Her friends barely believed he existed. She'd stopped talking much about him when all she'd gotten were skeptical eye rolls and *Raphael? Bailey, are you dating a Ninja Turtle?*

He'd never met them because he was so busy whenever he flew in. And then she wanted him all to herself. So yeah, she was giddy. She had a feeling she always would be.

"Bailey, shouldn't you be getting dressed?"

She frowned. She hadn't expected him to say that. She spent the night with him all the time when he came through town. "I thought…well." She swept a hand over her bare curves. "I'm ready for more if you are."

"I have an early flight out—I thought I told you."

He looked grim suddenly. She hated that grimness. It grabbed her by the throat and held her tight, filled her lungs with dread, and she couldn't quite pinpoint why. "No. You didn't." She forced a smile because there was no point fighting with him if these were their last few minutes together before he had to leave again. "You have to go back to Italy?"

"Yes," he said, reaching for his pants and tugging them on, covering up his gorgeous body.

She watched him dress the rest of the way, the reverse strip show still arousing even if it had a more depressing ending than the alternative.

His muscles rippled with each movement, his fingers blunt and efficient as he buttoned his shirt. Reminding her of just how *efficient* they were with her.

"Bailey," he said again, his tone vaguely…irritated. She couldn't recall Raphael ever being irritated with her before.

"I'm comfortable," she said, sighing heavily and rolling out of bed. "There. Now I'm not. I hope you're happy." She purposefully wiggled her hips a little bit as she made her way to where he'd torn her dress off earlier. "I hope this survived," she said, picking it up gingerly.

"I'll replace it if it didn't."

"I'm more worried about what I'll wear home." Another sigh escaped her lips. "When are you coming back?"

"I'm not."

She felt like all the air had been pulled from her body. She just stood there, blinking in the dim light, totally frozen while her fingers went numb and her insides went cold. "What do you mean, you aren't coming back?"

"I don't have any more work here in Vail. We're finished up with our meetings."

"Right. So. But… I'm here."

He laughed, a hard, low sound that wasn't like Raphael at all. "Sorry, *cara*, that is not enticement enough."

She was dumbstruck. Completely. And she hated herself for it. "I don't understand. We just had the nicest date and the best… I don't… I don't understand."

"It was goodbye. You have been an especially lovely diversion, but that's all it could ever be. I have a life back in Italy, and it's time I got back to it in earnest."

Dumbstruck turned into sucker punched. "A life? Are you… Raphael, are you married?"

"About to be," he said, his tone hard. "I can't afford distractions any longer."

"You're engaged. Of course you are," she said, words tumbling out of her mouth without her permission. "I bet you…live with her. Of course you only come and visit me every couple of months. I'm such an idiot."

She covered her mouth and stifled a scream. She was too angry to be humiliated. Too wounded to care if she bled all over him. "I was… I was a virgin, and you knew that," she threw at him. "I told you it was a big step for me!" Angry tears welled in her eyes, rolling down her cheeks.

"And I appreciated the gift, *tesorina*," he said, his tone now like iron. "We were together for eight months. It was hardly a fling."

"It's a fling if one of you isn't taking it seriously at all!" A sob rose in her throat, shaking her whole body. "If one of you knew it would end and was sleeping with someone else." She bent down then, picked up her shoe and threw it at his head.

He dodged it neatly, an Italian swear word on his lips.

She bent again, picking up her other shoe and flinging that at him too. This one hit him square in the chest. He closed the distance between them, grabbing hold of her wrist. "Enough." He released her as quickly as he'd taken hold of her. "Don't embarrass yourself, Bailey. Not more than you already have."

"You should be embarrassed," she said, her voice shaking. She pulled the dress on, then moved to pick her shoes up. She hadn't put her nylons back on, but who had the time for that ridiculousness when your heart had just been ripped out through your chest? "You are the one who *lied* to me." She sniffed much louder than she meant to, pulling her coat on over the dress, trying to ignore the fact that she was shaking so hard now her teeth were chattering.

"I never lied to you," he said, his dark eyes burning. "You created the story you wanted to believe."

She let out a feral growl and rushed past him, heading out the door as quickly as she could, feeling like a disgraced hooker walking out of his hotel room in the middle of the night, wearing high heels and a beautiful dress that she was going to have to burn now.

It wasn't until she was outside, until the cold wrapped itself around her, overtaking her, that she fell apart. Completely, utterly. She sank to her knees in the snow, sobbing until her throat hurt.

It felt like her life was over. And right now, she did not have it in her to put herself back together.

Three months later

I'm sorry, Bailey. But I can't have a waitress falling asleep in the kitchen in the middle of her shift. Especially not a fat waitress.

Her boss's voice played over and over in her head as she trudged back to her apartment. She had been right, that night three months ago when Raphael had broken things off with her. Her life pretty much felt like it was over.

She was so far behind in her classes it didn't look like she had the credits she needed to graduate, she didn't have a job anymore and she was so sick and tired she barely cared about either.

Now she was going to have to tell Samantha that she couldn't make rent. Well, this was the crowning achievement on the past months' humiliations, really. She had become everything she had felt so far above for most of her life.

When she had left home, left town, she had blistered her mother's ears with her rant about how she was off to make a better life for herself. One that wouldn't be all about men and an intense dedication to being a victim.

She'd gotten the hell out of metaphorical Dodge. Leaving behind that life of destitution. Where she'd been nothing but unwanted. Nothing but resented, and she'd vowed to do better.

She'd been wise to men, and what they might say to get into your pants, from the time she was way too young to know any such thing. Because she'd heard her mother rant at length on the subject after whatever boyfriend had broken up with her. As a result she had imagined herself as inoculated against such things. Had imagined that she was immune to that kind of behavior.

The truth of it was, she simply hadn't met a man who made her crazy enough. Then she met Raphael. And now, here she was, single, out of a job and pregnant. And all at the age of twenty-two.

She was the cycle. The cycle that she had so proudly and grandly told herself she wouldn't perpetuate. Now here she was. Perpetuating. She was a statistic. A sad statistic wandering around in the chilly, early spring air with nowhere in particular to go.

She stopped, turning to face the small general store across the street. Candy. She needed candy. Since she couldn't have wine. *Damn pregnancy.*

She ducked into the store and made her way to the nearest candy aisle, stopping abruptly when her eye caught the tabloid just above the chocolate bar her hand hovered over.

The man on the cover looked…far too familiar.

Prince Raphael DeSantis jilted by Italian heiress Allegra Valenti just weeks before royal wedding!

"What the actual *hell*?" The shoppers around her

startled when she all but shouted the words, but she didn't care. She reached out and grabbed the magazine, flipping through it with shaking fingers.

Raphael. *Prince* Raphael.

She flipped the pages until she saw it. The article about the scandal that was apparently rocking the principality of Santa Firenze, a tiny dot on the map of Europe. One she'd never even heard of.

It was him. There was no mistaking it. With his arresting good looks, more like a god than a man, and his incredible body...a body they had on show in the article, thanks to a few creeper beach pics. Those broad shoulders, washboard abs and lean hips...

She knew that body better than she knew her own.

"Oh, my..." She reached into her purse and pulled out a stack of tip money, throwing a ten down onto the counter. "Keep the change." She ran out with the candy bar and the magazine, her entire body starting to shake.

What *Twilight Zone* episode had she stumbled into? What kind of a joke was this?

By the time she got back to her apartment she felt like she was going to be sick all over the floor. And, given the theme of the last couple of months, she wouldn't be surprised if she did. Attempting to keep food down was sometimes a superhuman feat. Not that you could tell by her expanding waistline. Which her ex-boss had made clear to point out along with the firing.

She was tragic. So tragic that all she wanted to do was throw herself down on the bed and sleep for the rest of the day.

She made her way into the living room, where Samantha was sitting, looking wide-eyed.

"Are you okay?" Bailey asked, mostly to stave off the question of whether or not she was.

"You have a visitor," her roommate responded.

"Who?" she asked, feeling like the only possible option was that it was someone from the IRS telling her she owed back taxes, or maybe a police officer letting her know she had a warrant for a parking ticket she didn't know she had...something awful. Because that was the theme of the day. The theme of the past few months, really.

"*He's* here," Samantha said, sounding dazed.

There could only be one he. There was only one *he* that would make a woman's voice sound like that. Only one man Bailey had ever met who could render a woman completely stunned by his very presence.

And, as Bailey was processing that bit of information, she heard shoes on the hardwood floor and looked up, up into the dark eyes of Prince Raphael DeSantis just as he exited her bedroom.

He was here. In her crappy little apartment. Looking as out of place as a lion among house cats.

She wrapped her coat more tightly around herself, doing her best to conceal her figure. To hide the bump that she knew was pretty plainly visible without her woolen shield.

"What are you doing here?" she asked. She realized she was also still holding the tabloid with his face on it. She looked down at the magazine. Then back up at him. "What are you doing here?" she repeated.

"I came to tell you that I wanted to start seeing you again," he said.

"Oh, *please*." This exclamation came from her roommate, who had watched Bailey weep into her pillow for weeks now.

"What she said," Bailey affirmed, crossing her arms even more tightly beneath her chest.

"Could we have a moment?" He directed the question at Samantha, then, without waiting for a response, grabbed hold of Bailey's arm and guided her back into her bedroom. He closed the door, enclosing them both in the space.

And for a moment, she was completely lost in him. In his strength, in his very presence, which reached to every corner of the room, and around her. She wanted to lean into him. To rest her head against the solid wall of his chest and release hold of all of the heartbreak, fear and stress she had been enduring for the past few months.

She just wanted to fall into his arms and lose it all. Lose herself.

But that was impossible. He was…he was a liar. On so many more levels than she had realized.

"My engagement is off," he said, as though she were not holding a magazine in her hand proclaiming exactly that. "And, given that, I see no reason why the two of us can't resume our liaison."

"Our…*liaison*. The one where you come and visit me every couple of months for sex?"

"Bailey," he said, his tone exceedingly hard done by. It made her want to punch him. "I have a certain life, certain expectations, and…"

"These expectations?" She turned the tabloid around, thrusting it toward him. "You're a prince? What strange fairy tale did I fall into, Raphael? You said you were a pharmaceutical rep."

"You said I was a pharmaceutical rep, Bailey," he said. "Don't you remember?"

"I…" She remembered everything about the night she met him. The way that her world had stopped completely when their eyes had met. How out of place he looked in the sleazy diner that she worked at, Sweater Bunnies, where the waitresses all wore sweaters with plunging necklines and short shorts, with glittering tights and high heels.

His plane was delayed because of the weather. He had come into town on business. They had ended up talking. And then she had done something she had never done before in her life. She went home with him.

They didn't have sex. Not that first night. But he had kissed her, and she had…well, she'd learned an entirely new definition for the word *want*. Her entire body had caught fire with the touch of his lips, the touch of his hands. They had been talking one moment, and then the next, he had her down on the bed.

"I'm a virgin," she said.

"I don't need you to be," he responded, his voice rough, his hands tangled in her hair. "We don't have to play that game. Unless you want to."

"No," she said, "I really am. Like, a really, real virgin. Who has never done anything like this before, ever."

He sat up. "Never?"

"Never. But, I like you. And…maybe if the weather is bad tomorrow…"

"You want to wait, but you might be ready tomorrow?"

"I don't know."

"We'll wait," he said, kissing her cheek.

And he hadn't thrown her out. Instead, he had poured her a glass of soda and then continued to talk to her.

She hadn't made him wait long after that. The next night she'd made him her first, and she'd already been spinning fantasies about him being the only.

Then…well, then he'd turned out to be a frog. Except he was actually a prince. Which was just insane.

"Of course I remember," she snapped.

"Then you remember that you were the one who laughed at me, and said, 'You aren't a pharmaceutical rep or something, are you?' And I did not correct you. In fact, you will find, Bailey, that a great many of the things you think about me you created."

"So now you're gaslighting me? You're making this whole thing about what I chose to believe? And somehow, you think that will make me want you back. Not as a girlfriend, or anything like that, just as your little Colorado-based… Tell me, Raphael, where do your other women live?"

"I never thought of you that way," he said, his tone fierce. "Never."

"Actions speak louder than words and all of that. You treated me like one. You're still treating me like one. Get out of my apartment, Your Majesty," she spat.

"I am not in the habit of taking orders, you will find. I was all right playing your game before, but now you know. I am a prince, *cara mia*. And what I want, I have."

"Well," she said, flinging her arms out wide, "you don't get this."

He reached out, cupping the back of her head and drawing her forward. "You don't mean that."

"Oh, but I do." She pressed her hands flat against his chest—the better to shove him backward—only then he felt…so much like home. Like everything brilliant and perfect that she'd been missing while her life had been upended.

It was easy to forget he was the one who'd upended it.

He curved one arm around her waist, drawing her body flush against his. And then he frowned.

And she came back to reality, hard.

"Don't touch me," she hissed, pulling away and straightening her coat a little bit frantically.

She didn't want him to see that she was pregnant because…

Because she didn't know why. She'd resigned herself to her fate as a single mother because he was supposed to be married to someone else. Because the text she'd sent out to him after the fact saying she needed to talk to him had gone unreturned.

But he was here now. And he was a prince, damn it all.

Her own father had never been around, and she and her mother had suffered financially for it. Raphael could support their child. Could make sure they didn't struggle.

She flicked the top button of her coat open, her heart pounding. "I'm not going to be your lover, Raphael," she said, her voice trembling as she continued undoing buttons. She let her coat fall free and revealed the bump that was only just now visible beneath her tight-fitting sweater. "But whether you want to be or not, you are the father of my baby."

CHAPTER TWO

IT WAS RARE that Prince Raphael DeSantis was rendered speechless. But then, it was rare for him to be rejected.

And that had happened twice in the past week.

Were he a man with any insecurity, he might be wounded. However, he was the Crown Prince of Santa Firenze, a man who had been born with the world in hand and every advantage available to him. A man who—upon his birth—had been worshipped by the palace's many servants, simply because he existed. Reverence was a gift bestowed upon him from his first breath. And he had spent his life ensuring that he maintained the admiration of his people.

And this little waitress had refused him. Then gone on to reveal a surprise he certainly hadn't seen coming.

"You are certain it's mine?" He knew the question would earn him more of Bailey's ire, but he suddenly felt as though everything was hanging in the balance. This woman, who looked at him as though she wanted to do him bodily harm, was carrying the heir to the throne of his country.

She recoiled from him. "How dare you ask me that?"

"I would be remiss if I did not."

He tried to ignore the hurt in her blue eyes. This

changed things. It changed everything. Bailey had been
a diversion he wasn't looking for. And he had allowed
himself to get caught up in it. To enjoy the fiction that
she had built up around them. That he was a businessman, coming to Vail once every couple of months for
meetings and to spend time with her.

Somehow she hadn't seemed to know who he was.
But then, part of maintaining the admiration of his people had been keeping himself out of baser things like
tabloid news. Which he had clearly failed at recently.
He attributed that to his former fiancée, Allegra.

But it had all come to an end three months ago. He
had known that he couldn't continue his assignation
with Bailey right up until his marriage. He had never
touched Allegra, and he didn't love her, but he had intended to be a good husband to her. A faithful husband. Or at least—depending on the agreement they
ultimately reached—a discreet one.

When the engagement had ended, however, he had
immediately thought to come back to his mistress.

The world was crumbling as he knew it—a slight
exaggeration perhaps, but the cancellation of a royal
wedding could hardly be deemed insignificant. It had
made him tabloid fodder.

His father, the late ruler of Santa Firenze, had despised all forms of media and had felt it wholly beneath
a leader to become a headline when he should be aim-
ing to be part of history.

He had instilled this in Raphael, along with strength
and steel. There had been no softness allowed in his
childhood, and Raphael could see it for the benefit it
was now that he was a man, both of his parents long
dead and an entire nation left to him to oversee.

In fact, his marriage to Allegra was a testament to that strength. That he had been more than willing to set aside the desires of his flesh for the betterment of his kingdom.

Bailey, no matter that he desired her, could offer no political advantage to his country. Allegra, on the other hand, would bring an alliance with one of Italy's oldest families and a great deal of influence within the business community thanks to both her father and brother.

Bailey heated his blood. But his time with her was outside the norm…something separate from Santa Firenze. Something he could not afford to bring back there, he had known with certainty. Not only was she beneath him in status, she was a distraction. The sort his father had always warned against.

The only thing Bailey had…was his heir. And that was something that could not be ignored.

He had not foreseen this complication.

"Yes, Your Royal Jackass, it's your baby. Since you were the one to take my virginity, I would think you would know that."

"Nearly a year ago, Bailey. Many things could have happened since that first time we were together. I was not always here. And it has been three months since I left you. For all I know, in your grief, you sought solace with another man."

"Yeah, it's been a nonstop orgy since you dumped me. I figured, why not just go for it? After all, your royal scepter paved the way. Might as well allow the common folk a chance."

"Enough. You are being crude, and it doesn't suit you."

"Yes it does. It suits me perfectly. As you well know.

I am not the kind of woman that you could ever take back to your country, so you *must* think that. I'm a waitress. A lowly server that you met in a sleazy restaurant better known for the waitresses breasts than the chicken breasts. I would say this behavior suits me perfectly."

She was vibrating with rage, angry like she'd been the night he had ended things with her. When she had screamed at him, thrown a shoe at him. *Hit* him with a shoe. It had been the exact response he'd been looking for. He could not have her coming after him. Could not have her being tempted in any regard to find him, not when he was ready to get married and begin producing children. He had made their separation as devastating as possible so she would not seek him out.

Better to spoil her memory of him than leave her longing. Of course, he had changed his mind about that. Which he reserved his right to do. He was a prince, after all.

"You are carrying my child," he said, looking down at her stomach. She wasn't showing dramatically, just a vague bump beneath her sweater. Her curves looked a bit more abundant. He considered himself an expert on Bailey's curves, so he was certain his assessment was correct. "How far along are you?"

"Close to four months," she said. "It happened before we broke up. But I didn't know until after."

"Did you try and get in touch with me?"

That question seemed to make her angry, too. "Yes. I did. Though, since I didn't know your actual identity, it was a little bit tricky. I texted you."

The only number that Bailey had was to the phone that only she used. He had been careful to keep everything with her separate. Particularly when he had discovered that she truly didn't know who he was. There had been something so enticing about it. The chance to come here and be with a woman who had no expectations. To be more himself than any other venue allowed.

And when he had ended things with her, he had gotten rid of the phone. Cutting off his temptation. He didn't need to save messages from her. Or the occasionally suggestive photographs that she had provided.

"I no longer have that phone," he said.

"Wow. When you break up with a girl, you really go hard-core."

He frowned. "You keep using that word, Bailey. As though you were my girlfriend. From my point of view, we never had that kind of relationship." He realized, even as he spoke the words, that he was being extraordinarily unfair to her.

With most women, he laid out the ground rules from moment one. He had not been seeking Bailey out. Not at all. He had come to Vail to visit a friend's resort and see about investing in the property and its expansion. And then a blizzard had waylaid his travel.

Not even a man such as himself could control a storm.

He had wandered into a restaurant not far from his hotel, and had nearly walked right back out when he'd seen what sort of establishment it was. But then he had seen her. Somehow, in spite of the tacky surroundings, the horrendous uniform and the dim lighting, she had shone.

He had been able to think of only one thing. One word. *Mine.*

And there had never been a single thing in his life

that he had wanted and had not gotten. He had purposed in that moment that the waitress would be one
of them.

When she had made assumptions about who he was,
he had allowed her to do so. He had encouraged it. And
he had not done as impeccable a job as he usually did
of ensuring that the relationship stayed in the bedroom.
But he had reasoned that he only ever saw her for a
long weekend every couple of months. And it would
be wrong to keep her in a hotel room the entire time.

So he had taken her out. He had no connections to
Vail other than that one visit to see about investing.
The press never had any reason to take an interest in
him being there. Or even think that he would be there.

There were a great many advantages to having a
relatively low profile.

"What I mean," he said, attempting to soften his
tone, "is that I have lovers, not girlfriends. Women that
I carry out affairs with. I don't date. That's the issue
with being a prince. You cannot simply go public with
women, not without expectation being attached. However, I was hardly going to live my life celibate."

"You had a fiancée." The words were low, carrying
with them an edge of violence.

"Allegra was nothing more than a convenience. She
is from one of Italy's most revered families. She was
a reasonable choice for a man in my position. She was
not my lover."

"Well, I guess that's something," she said. "So. I
figure we need to come to some kind of child support
arrangement? I'm having your baby. If you need me to
get a paternity test, fine, whatever. I'll hate you, but
I already do. Whatever you need. A cheek swab, my

blood. Though I'd prefer not to give blood. I've already bled for you. I'm not doing it again."

"What are you talking about? A child support?"

"Presumably you have a castle. I would like to not live in a heap."

"And so you want money?"

He found her fascinating. This woman who had not known who he was. This woman who was standing there with a tabloid featuring him at her feet, who had been a virgin when he'd first taken her. Who was asking for child support, and not threatening to go to the press. Not demanding a pied-à-terre in various cities or pieces of the crown jewels.

Clearly, she had no understanding of the situation she found herself in, in spite of what she thought.

"I don't think it's unreasonable," she said. "My own mother was single. And my father didn't give us anything. I'm not going to consign my son or daughter to that life if I can make it better. I have a responsibility. And so do you."

"Undeniably I have a responsibility to this child, but I do not think you understand exactly what you're dealing with here," he said, staring at her, mystified.

"I'm dealing with an unexpected pregnancy and the best way that I can think to handle it. I want to make sure that you are not living in the lap of luxury while your son or daughter has nothing."

"Oh, I have no intention of my son or daughter lacking for anything. But if you think that I'm leaving them here in Colorado to be raised alone by you, you have failed to understand the man that you are involved with."

Her entire face turned pink, her rage seemingly

silent for the first time since he had aroused it three months ago.

"I am not sending child support checks, *cara*. There will be no more discussion of it."

"What do you mean you aren't allowing me to raise my child in Colorado? Under what authority? This is America! And last I checked, you probably aren't a citizen."

"Diplomatic immunity," he said, waving his hand, "and a desire to preserve relations with my country, will no doubt see any kind of court battle you should wish to wage fall in my favor. Who would give custody to a waitress from Sweater Bunnies when a prince is on hand to raise the child to rule?"

"You're going to take my baby from me?" Her voice had turned shrill, and he could see that she was looking around the room, her eyes darting back and forth. Probably looking for a weapon.

"It should not come to that."

"Start speaking slowly, and spelling out what exactly you're implying. Obviously I'm not picking up on it."

"Of course," he said, "there will be no discussion of my sending you child support checks, and no discussion of the child being raised here, because you will both be in Santa Firenze."

"I thought I wasn't fit to be brought back to your country."

She wasn't. Even now, looking at her, that intense possessiveness had him in a stranglehold. Taking her, claiming her seemed to be the most obvious choice.

Which was what gave him pause. A ruler was meant to be cool. A ruler was meant to direct his actions with his mind, his sense of honor, not with anything half as fickle as desire or heat.

He wondered what his father might have done in this instance. And then had to concede that his father would never have been so foolish as to get himself in this situation.

He was forced then to weigh his options. To bring back a woman such as this, one he had already decided was unsuitable for his kingdom…it was unfathomable.

But honor. Honor and duty were at the center of all of it, regardless of what she made him feel. His duty was to his child.

"That was before I knew you were carrying my heir." He took a step toward her, the word *mine* pounding itself through his head in time with the thundering of his heart. "Of course you are coming back to my country with me now. But not as my mistress. Bailey Harper, you are going to be my wife."

CHAPTER THREE

"You have a private jet."

"Of course I do," Raphael said, brushing past her and walking up the stairs into the sleek-looking aircraft.

"Were you in your private jet the night that we met?"

He treated her to a withering look. "I wasn't flying economy."

"I just…" She let the words trail off. There wasn't much to say. Not really. He was not the man she had thought he was. That had become apparent when he'd broken her heart the way that he had, when it had been revealed that there was another woman in his life. This was just another layer to it. She supposed that some people would view this as good luck. The fact that the man who had gotten her pregnant was wealthy, titled and powerful should be some kind of boon.

She looked up at the plane. She didn't really feel like it was a good thing. Not now.

She just felt small. Small and so desperately out of her depth.

She had argued with him about the marriage thing, and she intended to argue with him even more. But… what could be done? He presented a pretty ironclad case

when it came to how he would go about getting custody.
And she didn't want to lose her baby.

*Are you sure part of you just doesn't want to go off
with him because it sounds easy?*

She banished that traitorous voice, began to walk
up the steps and into the jet. And that feeling of being
tiny only increased. She was nothing. No one. Just a
girl from Nebraska who had gone to Colorado seeking
mountains and a fresh start. A girl raised by a single
mother in a drafty house built in the 1920s with a sag-
ging foundation and a crack in the ceiling.

She looked around the cabin, her jaw a little bit slack.
It was…she had never seen anything like this on the internet. She had idly scrolled through the odd slideshow
on various lifestyle websites showing the ridiculously
luxurious way that the rich and famous traveled, but
she had never imagined she would be standing in the
middle of it. Much less ready to fly on board.

"There are bedrooms back that way," he said, gesturing past the plush living area and bar to the back of
the plane. "There is also a bathroom and a shower."

"There's a shower?"

"Of course there is." And that was it. No further explanation. As if it really were the most typical thing on
the planet for a man to have a shower on his plane, and
she was the absurd one for thinking otherwise.

"Okay then. I will keep that in mind in case I feel a
little bit travel stale."

Her heart began to hammer loudly, her hands shaking as the door to the plane closed.

"You know," she said, "we don't have to go now. I
have… I have school to finish."

"You mentioned. In your rant as you packed your things."

She was failing right now, but still. "Well, it was a valid rant. I worked hard to pay my way this far through school, and if I don't finish this term, I'll be out the money for the classes."

He sat down on one of the tan leather couches, spreading his arms wide over the back, his posture laconic. She had to wonder how on earth she hadn't realized he was royalty. Sure, she had never been in the presence of anyone who could be considered royal, but he exuded it. How had she ever thought he was a normal man?

You never did. You saw him and the world stopped.

"Come now," he said, "*cara mia*, the cost of your college tuition will be the least of your concerns. I can arrange to have you complete your courses remotely. Or you may transfer to one of the universities in Santa Firenze. Of course, you will have to take classes at the palace and not on campus should you choose to do that."

"Why can't I go to the campus?"

"You would create a circus." He tapped the back of the couch with his fingertips. "I am not a man accustomed to getting tabloid attention. My family name has always been upheld, whispered reverently, spoken of with great respect. We are not part of the nouveau riche royal set who takes great pride in posting our social engagements on various online accounts. We take pride in the title. My father did before me, and I do it now. That headline you saw today was an aberration. There is a reason that you were not aware of my identity. I simply don't court publicity. That is the vocation of celebrity, and I am not a celebrity. I am the ruler of my country." He sighed heavily. "I dislike the position I find myself in. Because you…you will be a problem."

"Oh, will I? Excellent. One hopes that I will be too much of a problem for you to want to take on."

He waved a hand. "Not at all. You see, *cara*, you are carrying my baby. The most important thing on this earth is the birthright of that child. You must be married to me in order to secure that birthright."

She blinked. "Is this the Middle Ages?"

"No, this is Santa Firenze. And this is the cost of being royal."

"Good thing you're rich. It seems damned expensive."

"You have no idea. But, suffice it to say, your tuition is not my concern. In fact, it isn't your concern, either. You have no more financial concerns."

His words were strange. Made her ears feel fuzzy. She could hardly comprehend them. All she had worried about—from the time she had known what it was like to be hungry, from the moment she had experienced her first night in winter with the heat off because the electricity had been interrupted by the power company—was money. To have this man look at her, snap his fingers and say it was no longer a concern was…it was beyond surreal.

"I don't… I don't understand…any of this."

"It is simple," he said as the engines to the plane fired up and the aircraft began to glide down the runway. "I am a prince, I cannot have a bastard. I would have preferred a more suitable wife, a wife with a title or a pedigree of some kind. However, you are the one carrying my baby. That means I will have to make do with what I have."

"More flattering words have never been spoken, I'm sure."

"This is not about flattery. This is about reality."

The aircraft lifted off, and as it rose higher, Bailey's stomach sank into her feet. The longest plane ride she had ever been on was the short trip between Nebraska and Colorado. And nothing more. Which brought to mind other concerns. "Wait," she said, her heart kicking desperately against her chest, thinking that perhaps she had found a reprieve. "I don't have a passport."

He laughed. "That is of no concern to me. I can arrange to have one secured for you."

"Not by the time we reach your country."

"That is the thing. It is *my* country. No one is going to deny you admittance if I say you may have it. And as for coming back to the States, you certainly will eventually. So, we will secure you documentation for that eventuality. However, either way you'll be fine. You will be traveling with me."

He was maddening. Nothing fazed him. Nothing even made him pause. He was going about this with all the ruthless efficiency of a commander going into battle. And each and every protest issued from her lips, he struck down like an enemy of war.

"Does none of this bother you?" she asked. "I mean, you say you don't like being in the tabloids, but you say it with all the fire and passion of an iceberg. Meanwhile, I feel like my life is falling apart. I feel like I've been dropped into some third-rate reality show."

"That's insulting. This is first-class," he said, his tone dry, "all the way."

"Is this a joke to you? Your life has been easy, I get that. It radiates off you in waves. Your privilege. Your

wealth. Everything I've had I've worked for. Every day
of my life has been infused with some kind of struggle.
Every single thing I own was purchased at great cost.
You spend more on bottled water in a week than I spend
on groceries in a month."

"That is probably true. But now this is your life. Do
not worry about your roommate, by the way. I made
sure to give her several months of rent so that she would
not feel your absence too keenly."

"Nice of you to consider her feelings," she said,
though she was grateful that Samantha wouldn't be left
high and dry. Suddenly a wave washed over her, leaving
her feeling adrift. Weightless. "I think I'm in shock,"
she said, sinking further back into the chair across from
him, her limbs suddenly feeling very shaky.

"Bailey," he said, his expression concerned. "Are
you able to breathe?"

She laid her head back, feeling dizzy.

"No," she said.

Suddenly he was next to her, his large hands cupping
her face. He was warm, and he was so very Raphael.
"Bailey," he said, his tone stern. "Keep breathing."

Her vision went fuzzy around the edges for a second, then dark…

It came back, with too much clarity, too much brightness. She felt sick to her stomach, a cold sweat on her
forehead, her fingers icy. "What happened?" she asked.

"You passed out," he responded. He looked…he
looked genuinely concerned. Though she wondered if
it was for her or for the baby.

"Don't touch me," she said, pulling away from him.
He complied, removing his hands from her face. She
hated it. Hated that when he touched her she still felt

something. Hated that he wasn't touching her anymore. Hated herself for caring.

"Have you been passing out regularly?"

"No," she said, trying not to watch him as he stood up and crossed to the bar. Trying very, very hard not to pay total and complete attention to his every movement. "I've had a little bit of a shocking day. I walked into a grocery store and saw that my ex-lover was a prince. Seeing as I knew I was having his baby, it suddenly occurred to me that I was having a prince's baby. Then I went home, and said prince was in my bedroom. Then he dragged me onto a private plane, all the while demanding that I marry him or he'll take my baby away. I think I'm just suffering the aftereffects."

He opened up a bottle of sparkling water and poured it into a glass, his movements deft and swift. Then he crossed the space to her, handing her the drink. "I found out I was going to be a father today, and I seem to be handling it well."

"Because you're a robot," she replied, taking a sip of the bland, fizzy liquid.

"I think that you can attest to the fact that I'm all man, Bailey. Not a robot."

"Not all. Parts of you," she said. "You seem to have Tin Man syndrome. No heart."

"I love my country," he responded, his tone cool. "I am eternally loyal to it. And I will do whatever is necessary to preserve the legacy. There is no reason for me to panic about the situation we find ourselves in. There is no question that I must marry the mother of my child. And while who you are will require a little bit of damage control, I was already set to be married in the next month. And, presumably, sometime after my wife would have given birth to a child. That has always been the course plotted out before me. All in all, only the bride has changed."

"So…women and the children they bear are interchangeable to you?" she asked.

"A wife and child are necessary components to my life," he said, his tone hard. "Essential to the continued health of the kingdom and bloodline. The importance cannot be overstated."

"But who the woman…"

"Matters in terms of bloodline, political affiliation and the ability to have children. You have one out of three—I think you're smart enough to guess which."

He said it with such calm. As though the bride were the most incidental part of the marriage. As though he didn't care at all whether he was married to her or to the shiny brunette she'd seen in the tabloids. "You're horrible. Just horrible. How did I manage to convince myself for eight months that you were Prince Charming? No reference to your *actual* royalty intended."

"We see what we want to see, Bailey. You wanted to see me as something that I wasn't. It was convenient for you at the time. I was an easy lover for you to have. Don't pretend that it didn't suit you on some level to be with a man who was only around part of the time."

"Or I was an idiot virgin who had finally found a man that she wanted to sleep with, and had her judgment completely clouded by her orgasms."

Her words hung between them, tense and heavy. She despised herself for bringing that up. For bringing up the pleasure they had found together. She would rather forget it. It kept her up at night. All day, she would drag herself around, feeling exhausted and heartbroken. But night was worse. Because then she would dream. And when she dreamed, it was that Raphael was in bed with her. Touching her, kissing her. And when she woke up, she was alone. Hideously, depressingly alone, and she ached. For a touch she would never have again.

"I am sorry you were hurt," he said, his tone clipped. "That was never my intention. But I have known who I was to be, what sort of woman I was to marry, from the time I was a boy."

"And that woman isn't me."

"No." He pushed his hand through his dark hair. "It is important to make the best choices I can for my country. And someday my child will do the same. It is what was instilled in me from the beginning. My mother reinforced my father. She had been raised to be the wife of a prince, and she knew her place. That is what it takes to raise the heir to a throne, Bailey. You must understand it is not snobbery on my part—at least not entirely—when I say you are not suited."

"I…" She swayed slightly in her seat. "I really don't even know how to have this conversation."

"You should get some rest," he said, stunning her with that declaration. "When we land we will be very close to the palace, and you can get settled in. In the meantime, I am afraid that you are overtaxed."

"I don't feel like you've earned the right to comment on my level of taxation."

"As ruling government of an entire nation, taxation falls under my purview."

"Oh, well, that's fabulous. I guess we know which things are certain. Death, taxes and Raphael."

"I'm hardly going to kill you, *cara*. I'm going to make you a princess."

Suddenly, she felt so tired she could barely hold her head up. She could not be a princess. She was a waitress. And waitresses didn't become princesses. "I'm going to have that nap now."

Bailey wandered to the back of the plane, opening the door to the bedroom, then closing it tightly behind her. It was bigger than her bedroom in her apartment. With a large, ornate bed that looked like it was designed for much more than sleeping. It was ridiculous. *He* was ridiculous. This whole thing was ridiculous.

She kicked her shoes off, crossing to the bed before throwing herself down on her face like some tragic cartoon princess. She shut her eyes tight, trying not to give in to the tears that were building behind them.

This had to be a dream. All of it. When she woke up in the morning, her head would be clearer. She would be single, alone and pregnant. Her ex-boyfriend would be nothing more than that jerk pharmaceutical rep from Italy who had left her in the lurch. He would absolutely not be the prince of some obscure country, and she would not be a future princess.

The alternative was unthinkable.

When they disembarked in Santa Firenze, Raphael had them pull the car right up to the plane. He was feeling more than slightly concerned for Bailey's health. Or, at the very least, the health of their unborn baby.

She had been especially pale ever since he had first seen her in her apartment, and she had gotten only more waxen as the trip had worn on. Though he had only seen her once after she had gone to the bedroom to sleep, and that was only to use the restroom about a half hour before they landed.

He was confused by her. By their every interaction. She was not grateful for the offer of marriage. Not especially pleased that he was giving her the chance to be a princess. His wife. A position of great honor. One that most women would fight over.

And yet the two who'd had it offered to them both seemed to have rejected it.

Allegra was a separate issue.

"The car is waiting," he said through the closed bathroom door.

Bailey emerged a moment later, wet-haired, gritty-eyed and cranky, wearing a university sweatshirt and a pair of stretch pants.

"I see you availed yourself of the shower," he said.

"How often do you get a shower at thirty thousand feet? I thought that if I didn't at least give it a try, I would be seriously failing in the luxury stakes."

"Well, you will have ample opportunity to use the facilities again. Even if I upgrade jets, it will still have a shower."

"You're assuming that I will be making use of your jet in the future."

"Of course, you're marrying me. Pretending otherwise is ridiculous." He grabbed hold of her elbow, leading her from the plane, carefully helping her down the steps. "Now, come get in the car."

She sputtered, "Just because you say nothing else makes sense does not mean that nothing else makes sense."

He opened the door to the car, gesturing for her to get in. She shot him a deadly glare, then complied. He got in beside her, slamming the door shut. "You seem to be misunderstanding," he said, feeling very much like he was speaking a different language. Because Bailey seemed to persist in misunderstanding him. "I am the ruler of Santa Firenze. No one in my family has produced an illegitimate child. Not one. No one in my family has ever been divorced. We are a hallowed and storied lineage. I am offering you a chance to become part of it. The fact that you have rejected me is outrageous on so many levels I cannot even begin to list them all."

"By all means," she said, leaning back in her seat. "List them. If you have time."

"It isn't that long of a drive to the castle."

She blinked. "Castle?"

"What part of *prince* are you having trouble comprehending? I speak very good English, though Italian is my first language. You, however, are making me question my linguistic skills."

"I would hate to be the cause of you questioning your linguistics. I'm sure that they're fantastic."

"They can't be overly fantastic, because you do not seem to understand anything of what I am telling you." There was no point arguing.

She would understand the moment his family home came into view. It was the jewel of Santa Firenze. Settled in the middle of the Alps, overlooking one of the deepest and bluest lakes in Europe, craggy peaks rising up around it. She would understand then. What he was offering. Understand what a gift he was presenting her with.

As the car made its way down the narrow, winding two-lane road, Bailey insisted on shifting constantly in her seat and letting out long, huffy sighs.

"Your distress is noted," he said.

"Not overly. You keep accusing me of not understanding, and yet I think you're the one who has not fully taken on board that I am not happy about this."

"I am offering you marriage. Legitimacy for your child, an end to your financial concerns."

"About that," she snapped. "Where was your offer to end my financial concerns when I was working double shifts at that horrible restaurant? As I was killing myself to get through college, and you were presenting yourself as a businessman there on your company's dime?"

"Would you have accepted my offer of financial assistance?"

Her face went blank then, her mouth settling into a stubborn line. "Yes," she said.

"You're a terrible liar. You would not have accepted. Not from Raphael the businessman. And you seem to like Raphael the prince a lot less."

"That's because the first time I met Raphael the prince was when he was breaking up with me at midnight after what I had thought was a very romantic date. Only then you threw me out into the snow."

"I wanted a clean break. I felt it was better for both of us."

"Don't try to convince me that you lost any sleep over any of that."

He *had*. She had no idea. He had lost countless hours of sleep, lying there hard and aching, wanting something that only she could give to him. She had cast a spell over him from the moment he had first seen her, and he had never been able to explain it. He only knew that she affected him in a way no other woman ever had. And it had nothing to do with skill.

He could remember the first time she had knelt

down before him and taken him into her mouth. The way that she had tasted him, with shy, timid strokes of her tongue, how she had taken him in as deep as she could, her every movement uncertain. It was not her skill that enticed, but her sincerity. Her intense dedication to him. He was a man who had always felt a certain level of worship was his due, but it meant so much more coming from such a willing supplicant, rather than a trained one.

So yes, he had lost sleep. He'd had no desire to touch another woman, and, in fact, that had worked to his advantage, since he had purposed that he would not until his wedding night with Allegra. In that time he had attempted to drum up some kind of enthusiasm for the woman he was engaged to. But he had found none. Allegra was beautiful, with golden skin and dark, shimmering curls.

But he had craved the pale, flaxen-haired beauty of Bailey.

It was all vaguely ridiculous. He was fantasizing about a university student named *Bailey*. Princess Bailey.

But that was the thing with honor. It was supposed to matter even if it was hard. A truly strong oak didn't bend in the wind, and neither could the ruler of Santa Firenze.

As a boy, when he'd hurt himself, his father had not allowed his mother or the servants to comfort him. It had been up to him to breathe through the pain and carry on. That, his father had told him once, was how a man learned to soldier on in all things. If you could do it with a cut, you would do it with an emotional wound, too.

When he was older, his father had told him it applied to other physical aches, as well. A man might want a certain woman, might burn for her, but if there was potential a dalliance would harm the country, that craving—like all other harmful desires—had to be cast aside.

The prince of Santa Firenze could have whatever his heart desired. And that was why his heart, soul and sense of honor had to be made strong.

Raphael knew that he was strong. Had been, utterly and completely all his life.

Until her.

It was *truly* ridiculous. But here they were. And she, somehow, felt like she was in a position to play hardball.

The limo wound itself around the last curve, and, finally, the stately palace gates came into view. Wrought iron and scrolling, the family crest emblazoned upon them. They parted for the car as if by magic, and the limo rolled through a lane lined with hedges until they reached the magnificent courtyard in front of the palace.

The ground was overlaid with brick. A giant fountain dominated the center. At its top was a golden statue and there were many others fashioned from marble all around, representing the great leaders of his country. His very bloodline carved into stone in front of this hallowed castle that had housed generations.

He looked over at her and was satisfied to see that, finally, she had the decency to look impressed. She was staring up at the castle, at its turrets, with ivy climbing up the side and the blue-and-white flags of his country waving in the breeze from the very top of the shining palace.

"This is my home," he said, stating the obvious for

dramatic effect. "And when you are my wife, it will be your home. When our child is born, it will be his home. Do you still think you should raise him in an apartment in Colorado with your roommate?"

"I... I had no idea."

"It is not my fault you don't pay attention to current affairs. Or perhaps it is my fault, for keeping my country financially sound and free of most of the conflicts that happen in the world. We have very few reasons to be in the news because the citizens are happy, the coffers are full and we have no national security crises or natural disasters to speak of."

"Is this Narnia?"

"If it were, then a breath would turn all of the statues back to flesh. However, it is the real world. And they are only stone."

"That's a shame," she said. "Then all I would have to do is walk back to the wardrobe and I could be free of you."

She was mutinous. And he had never dealt with mutiny before. Like his father before him, he'd made Santa Firenze his life. Nothing had ever come before it. And as such, no one in his country had ever had cause for complaint.

"You don't actually want to be free of me," he said. How could she? "You're putting up a fight because you have an idea of what your life should be. I would argue that you are putting up a fight additionally because you have an idea of what consequences you should suffer for your sins."

"My sins?" she asked.

"Yes," he said, "your sins. You think you should be punished for this. Because you allowed yourself to get pregnant. And now you must pay penance. The sad, single mother, waiting tables, having been abandoned by her lover. It's a very nice narrative, but it is not a situation you find yourself in. You have a man willing to step up and take responsibility. More than a man, you have a prince. Saying anything but an emphatic yes is a waste of your resources."

She looked up at the palace, her eyes wide, her lips parted slightly. He was struck in that moment by the fullness of her beauty. Just as he had been the first time he'd seen her. And now she was carrying his child. She would be his wife.

Mine.

He pushed that word to the back of his mind. This wasn't about that. It was a necessity. What he must do. It had nothing to do with want. With that thing Bailey made him feel that was so perilously close to weakness.

"Come," he said, opening the door and extending his hand to her. "We must get you to your room."

CHAPTER FOUR

BAILEY TRIED NOT to stare too gauchely as she entered the palace, her heart thundering loudly. Loudly enough that she was pretty sure it was echoing off the marble walls of the massive antechamber they were standing in now. She had never seen anything like this in her life. It was like something out of a movie, except in a movie she had a feeling she would be heading toward some sort of fun montage where she would try on lots of dresses and upbeat pop music would play in the background while a sassy stylist told her how amazing she looked.

Instead, she was standing there wearing nothing more than a sweatshirt and pants that had seen better days, feeling like something a very large, overly self-satisfied cat had dragged in.

There were servants wandering around the palace, not making eye contact with Raphael, as though any unsolicited contact would be far too presumptuous on their part.

They did not look at her, either. Not with any kind of curiosity. In fact, she seemed beneath their notice. As though she were merely a package he had brought in after a day of shopping.

"It's so quiet in here," she said, her voice reverberating around them even though she was speaking softly.

"There are so many people in the palace at all times, it would be difficult to think if everyone were carrying on a conversation, don't you agree?"

"So you have a…silence policy?"

"There is no policy. But my father was one to train the servants to ensure they were rarely seen and rarely heard. I have done nothing to revise that code of conduct, as it suits me." He, on the other hand, didn't seem to feel like he was speaking too loudly. His voice echoed across the room, and he was not bothered by it in the least.

"You are definitely an *elevated* personage," she said, following him just slightly behind. "Aren't you?"

"This is my palace," he said, making a broad, sweeping gesture. "Of course I am elevated."

"It's just… I had the feeling royalty was a bit more modern nowadays. Prince Harry is out greeting soldiers and things."

"And getting caught with his trousers down at hotels in Las Vegas."

"We both know your trousers have been down, Raphael—it's just that nobody was there to take pictures. Actually, I could have taken pictures. I should have. I sent you some scandalous shots and sadly, never got a nude pic from you. Think of the leverage that would provide me."

His eyes sharpened. "I see you're finally considering the angle of using the press against me."

"I don't want to. Not particularly. To what end? So that we're both embarrassed? So that our child can look at the headlines in the future and see all the ugly things we said about each other? That isn't what I want. We both know that even if I were able to disgrace you by giving sordid details of your secret affair with a waitress, I would be the one who was called a whore."

"You speak the truth," he said, resting his hand on the solid marble banister, one foot on the first stair. "That is how it has always been."

"Yes, indeed," she snapped.

He arched a dark brow. "Don't look so angry with me," he said. "I don't rule over the whole world."

She sniffed. "You act like it." He continued up the stairs. She followed. "What about my things?"

"They are being handled. Though I sincerely doubt that any of your things will be deemed suitable for your new position."

She thought of her collection of clothing, all relatively dear to her, since she was a pretty intense bargain shopper who saw the experience as something of a covert ops situation. "I like my clothes."

"You will have new clothes. Better clothes. More than you could possibly wear."

"I don't understand the point of all of this."

"The point is that you are to be my queen. And you will look like my queen. When we break the news of our impending marriage, it will be with the view of presenting you in the best way possible. It does not benefit me to embarrass you, either."

"Well, at least there's that." Her stomach sank, tightening a little bit. "I don't…what is all of this going to entail?"

"You have seen movies where the people stand out on the balcony and wave at their subjects below?"

"Of course. It's a cliché."

He didn't miss a beat. "Prepare to become a cliché."

She took the steps quickly, trying to keep up with him. "You can't be serious. We're not really going to… that isn't…you don't expect to present me to the entire nation."

"Don't be silly," he said, and she felt herself start to breathe again. "I will be presenting you to the entire *world*."

Her heart slammed against her sternum. "The *entire world*? The entire world isn't going to care about me. I'm just… Bailey Harper from Nebraska. And two days ago I was a waitress."

"That is exactly why the world will be interested in you," he said, his tone fierce. "They will hold you beneath greater scrutiny than they ever would have held Allegra. They will turn over your every potential scandal. They will bring up the fact that you were waiting tables in a restaurant designed to flaunt the female figure. They will bring up the fact that you were pregnant prior to our marriage. The fact that I very likely had to marry you. They will find out the details of your childhood, of your parentage, and they will use it against you. Because that is what the media does."

"You make it all sound so exciting," she said, deadpan, trying to keep the abject horror out of her voice.

"It is simply the truth," he said. "It is why I have done my very best to stay on the right side of things. But I cannot do anything about the fact that this is going to create a scandal."

"What if I just went back to Colorado? What if we just…forget this happened."

He stopped again, turning to look at her, his eyes

fierce. "I cannot forget this happened," he growled. *"Ever."*

"But you could marry a more suitable woman. And you could kind of do it like they did back in the days of yore. You know, pay off your mistress, pretend that your bastard doesn't exist. That's kind of the way they did it, right?"

"It is not the way *I* do it. I am a man who is more than able to own his mistakes."

"Oh," she said, "excellent. I get to be something you own. A mistake you own, even. I'm the luckiest girl in the world."

"Whether or not you realize that, you are," he returned. "You are to be my princess—is there something degrading about that in your eyes?"

"No, there is something degrading about being seen as so far beneath someone that they lie to you about who they are, keep you as their dirty little secret, then abandon you so that they can marry someone who's more suitable, only bringing you back to their country when they realize that you are pregnant with their baby. None of this has anything to do with me. So why would you expect me to be flattered?" The words came hard, fast.

She didn't even know why she was so angry, because she shouldn't care. She should be happy, come to think of it. She should be happy that she didn't have to worry about the future of her child. That she wouldn't be destitute, waiting tables for the rest of her life. That she could give her baby something more than the kind of unstable situation she'd had growing up.

Except she didn't feel triumphant. Because at the end of the day, she hadn't really broken the cycle. She had still fallen into it. It was just that she had gotten pregnant with Raphael's baby, and not some random auto mechanic she'd met while passing through a dusty town in the Midwest, as her mother had done.

Bailey had just been more fortunate in her mistake, that was all. She couldn't feel triumphant about it. She couldn't feel anything but stupid.

"We will argue no more," he said, his voice hard. Then he turned and continued on up the stairs.

She let out a hard breath and followed after him. "Does the staircase ever end?" she asked.

He said nothing. Rather he let the answer become self-evident when they reached the top and a grand corridor opened up in front of them. Art that looked to be painted by the masters hung on the walls, various suits of armor positioned between each grand painting. The place was a museum, from the intricate scrollwork carved into the stone to every painting, every artifact displayed throughout.

"Your room is just here," he said, opening up a set of broad blue double doors that revealed a lavish sitting area that graduated up to a bedroom set. The bed itself had a velvet canopy that hung down and enough pillows stacked on top of the plush bedspread that it looked like it was prepared to accommodate an entire harem.

"Just how many people are supposed to sleep in that bed?"

He said nothing. Instead, he simply looked at her. And it burned all the way down to her toes.

"I didn't—"

"You have your own bathroom, shower and bath, as well," he said, cutting her off. "And this door here connects to my room, which shall make things convenient for us."

Her heart stopped cold. "How will it be more *convenient* for us, Raphael?"

"We are to be man and wife, *cara*. There are certain expectations that go along with that."

She seriously thought her head might explode. His outright arrogance knew no bounds. She was astounded. *Enraged.*

"You honestly think I'm going to sleep with you?"

"You have done so before," he said, gesturing toward her midsection.

"Yes," she said, "I did. When I thought you were a normal man. A man with a heart. A man that I might have a future with."

"Clearly you have a future with me. We are to be married."

"We are to be married only because your fiancée dumped you at the last minute." She took a step toward him, seething. "Only because I'm carrying your child. And had your fiancée not broken things off, you wouldn't even know that I was having a baby, because you never bothered to respond to my text."

"As I told you before, I had gotten rid of the phone you used to contact me."

She blinked. "And a prince wasn't concerned about missing calls or texts going to an old number?"

"It was a phone that was only for you," he responded.

"A burner phone." She shrieked the words. "You had a burner phone for me. I really was your filthy secret, wasn't I? What would have happened if people had discovered your assignation with me? How *humiliated* you would have been." She laughed, and once she started she had a hard time stopping. It wasn't funny. It cut her down deep. But it was either laugh or curl into a ball and weep. "Well, now the entire world is going to know. Funny how things work out, isn't it?"

"I am going to do my best to make it as painless for both of us as possible."

"You're a saint, Raphael," she spat. "You really are. But if you think you're a saint that's getting anywhere near my body again, you are fooling yourself."

"I don't understand what the issue is. We share a mutual attraction…"

"I trusted you," she said, her voice low, vibrating. "I trusted you with my body, and you knew that cost me. I didn't even know who my father was," she said, "and I was determined that I would never be like my mother. That I would make better decisions. Instead, I met you. And you set out to make sure that I became exactly like her. I don't trust you anymore." Her voice was trembling now. "I don't think I will ever trust you again. I will marry you, Raphael. I will marry you because it is truly the best thing for our child. I will marry you because I don't know what else to do. Because I want this baby, because I want to not be a waitress forever. Because I don't want my child to go to bed hungry, to go to bed cold. For those reasons, I will marry you. But I will not be your wife. Not really."

His face hardened, his eyes growing cold. "Do you expect me to be celibate for the rest of my life?"

"I don't care what you do. As long as you don't come anywhere near me."

"We shall see," he said, his tone made of pure ice now.

"There is nothing to see," she said. "My decision is made. And unless your particular brand of bastardry extends to forcing women into bed with you, I can safely say that you will not be having me in yours ever again."

"I have never had to force a woman into my bed," he gritted out, "you least of all. The reason I said *we shall see* is that I hold out very little hope for your self-control, *cara*. I believe that I can have you begging for me with the proper flick of my wrist between those pretty thighs."

She ignored the desperate well of longing that opened up inside her, making her conscious of how empty she was, of how lonely. Of just how much she desired him. "Never," she said, tilting her chin up.

He said nothing. Instead, dark eyes burning into hers, he closed the space between them, wrapping his arm around her waist, his grip like an iron bar. He looked... she could see almost nothing of the man she had known in Vail. This was the prince. Commanding, ruthless and so beautiful she could scarcely breathe for it.

Perhaps this was more evidence of just how weak she was. Or perhaps it was simply a testament to Raphael. Either way, she found herself looking back at those black, fathomless eyes, desire yawning through her, stretching all the way down to her toes, hitting everyplace in between.

It didn't matter that only a few hours ago she felt like she was near death. It didn't matter that she was wearing nothing but stretch pants and a ratty sweatshirt. It didn't matter that her hair was unkempt, unstyled, and that any makeup left behind was a mere ghost of what had been applied the night before. Nothing mattered but this. But him holding her, and her wanting him.

Before she had a chance to protest, before she had a

chance to even consider if she might want to, his lips crashed down on hers.

It was as fast as it was ruthless, a claiming of her mouth that mirrored the way he had stormed back into her life today. Taking ownership, making her his.

She left her arms at her sides at first, and then she could no longer resist. She clung to him, curling her fingers around the soft fabric of his shirt, holding tightly to him, because if she didn't, she would fall to the ground.

Three months.

Three months she had been without this. Without him. It was so much better than she remembered. So much more.

And then he released her, his top lip curling. "As I said. We shall see."

Then he turned and walked out of the room, leaving her there with her shame and with a burning desire that refused to be quenched no matter how much her brain and her heart tried to put it out.

CHAPTER FIVE

THE NEXT MORNING when Bailey did not appear for breakfast, Raphael went in search of her. She was not in her bedroom. Which was a surprise. He had expected to find her there, sleeping late, as Bailey had often done when she had spent nights in the hotel with him. But she was nowhere to be found. He wandered the halls, wondering if there was any way she had possibly made an escape. And to what end. She must know that he would find her. There was nowhere on earth she could go to hide from him. As evidenced by this morning's headline, the paparazzi had already identified her as his potential lover. And were speculating about whether or not she figured into his breakup with Allegra. She was not anonymous. Already she was conspicuous.

And he had almost infinite resources. There was no way she could avoid him for too long.

He remembered then that she had no passport. And his lips curved into a smile. She could go no farther than the borders of his country. And that meant he wouldn't have to cast a very wide net at all to find her.

One of his servants rushed by, her eyes downcast.

"Where is Bailey?" he asked.

The woman stopped and looked up, her expression

serene. "Ms. Harper is taking her breakfast in the library."

Well, he had to give her full marks for knowing exactly who he was talking about and where she was.

"Thank you," he returned. He made his way down the corridor, flinging the doors wide when he reached the library. Bailey, who was settled into an armchair with a book in her hand, startled.

"How did you know I was here?"

"I have staff."

"Yes, I am aware of that. They're the ones who brought me breakfast," she said, lifting up a cup. "And tea. They're all very nice. Maybe you should talk to them instead of ignoring their very existence unless you have a pronouncement."

"I do not ignore them. They maintain distance out of respect. If I were to stop and speak to each and every one of them, no one would get any work done, myself included. I am a fair ruler and a very good employer. They do not need me to co-opt their time in order for them to feel that. Just as I do not need fawning to know that they revere me."

"Wow," she said. "You're…a whole thing."

"So very nice of them to aid you in hiding away in my home," he continued as though she hadn't spoken.

"I'm not hiding. It's just that this place is the size of a small city. I practically need a cab to get across it."

"Dramatic as ever. I have taken the liberty of procuring you a new wardrobe."

She set her teacup down. "Like…you personally?"

"Don't be ridiculous."

"Right. Well, you procuring me a wardrobe is somehow not ridiculous?"

"There is nothing ridiculous about me."

She laughed. "Are you kidding me?" Bailey stood, stretching, the soft fabric of her T-shirt conforming to her breasts and to the soft swell of her stomach as she did. "You, who were carrying on a secret affair with a university student in Colorado but is secretly a prince with a castle and a superiority complex that would suggest you have little going on in your…trouser region."

"Well, we both know that isn't true."

She waved a hand. "I have nothing to compare it to."

"Regardless, you know every inch of me. And know I am not ridiculous." Her cheeks turned a deep shade of pink, and he felt an answering fire in his gut.

"That's one man's opinion," she said, her tone arch.

"The only opinion that matters in this country."

"Ridiculous," she muttered.

"The press conference will be today."

"What?" she asked. "I'm…jet-lagged still."

"It cannot be helped. The wedding must take place as quickly as possible. I'm sure you understand that."

"But weddings take time to plan?" It was phrased as a question, her voice slightly tremulous.

"Not when you have infinite wealth and power."

"Well, I really wouldn't know anything about that."

He frowned. "No. Nor will you. But we should discuss your monthly stipend. It will be quite generous, of course."

"I…" She blinked. "I don't know what to say to that."

"You'll need your own card, naturally. You will want to shop. Dine out with friends."

"Are you offering me an allowance like a child?"

"No," he said. "I am offering some independence."

"To spend your money. At least, an amount you determine is acceptable."

"I can give you a credit card without a limit, conversely. I'm not worried about your spending habits. You're a *terrible* gold digger, Bailey. You failed to recognize you had hooked yourself a prince. Then you didn't go to the tabloids, and when I mentioned you were getting a new wardrobe your eyes did not glitter with anything like triumph. In fact, you look slightly like you want to kill me."

She pursed her lips in thought. "*Kill* is a strong word. I don't want to kill you. *Maim*, possibly."

"Well, that is reassuring. I would try to keep jokes about harming my royal personage at a minimum around my Secret Service. They take a dim view on that."

She cocked her head to the side. "Where were they when you were with me?"

"As I told you already, I have a fairly low profile. If I don't want to be recognized, casual dress and a pair of sunglasses generally does it."

"The Clark Kent of royalty."

He frowned. "Excuse me?"

"Because nobody recognizes that you're Superman when you have your glasses on."

He found himself laughing, which caught him by surprise. That was more like the relationship he'd had with her before. She always had a way of amusing him, often when he least expected it. They should have nothing to talk about. He had often thought that when the two of them had been together. And it wasn't because he wanted to get to know her that he had initially pursued that connection with her.

Attraction. That was what had hit him upon first seeing her. Need. Want.

He had expected to sleep with her. What he hadn't expected was to spend hours talking to her. And enjoying those conversations.

A man in his thirties, raised to be royalty of a small country in Europe, should have little in common with a university student in her twenties from the United States. And perhaps they didn't have much in common. But she intrigued him. She surprised him. And he found he quite enjoyed it.

Surely, since she was going to be his wife, that was okay.

"I suppose that's true," he said. "I didn't make any announcements about coming into the States. I was there to visit a ski resort owned by a friend. And see about investing. That night, as you know, there was a blizzard, and I was unable to fly out."

"Then, to paraphrase, of all the diners by the airport, why did you walk into mine?"

"I nearly walked back out. I didn't realize what sort of establishment it was. And while I was reasonably confident no one from the press was nearby, I cannot take the chance that I might be seen somewhere of that nature. But then I saw you."

Color rose in her cheeks. "I made you stay?"

"I wanted you," he said, his voice rough. "From the moment I saw you."

He didn't know what he had expected. Really, he needed to stop expecting anything when it came to Bailey. She did not behave in any way that made logical sense to him. But he did not expect for her to frown.

"You make it sound like I was a watch."

"You're going to have to clarify," he said, his tone dry.

"Like, you saw me, and you wanted to buy me. Like I was something you might see in a store."

She wasn't wrong. It was the exact same thing to him. He wanted something, he got it. Women were no exception. Much like watches or cars. All of them were expensive, and often a lot of trouble. And yet he went to great lengths to acquire them. He didn't see how that was offensive.

"People are not things," she said, her tone hard, her expression matching it. As though she had been able to read his thoughts.

"Perhaps not. But things have value. It is not the insult you make it sound like."

"You're not supporting your case."

"I do know that people are not things," he said. Still, the acquisition of things, favors or the affections of women all often went much the same for him. What he saw, he soon had.

"I'm skeptical."

"You are welcome to remain skeptical. However, we must get you ready for today's conference. We have three hours. I have someone coming in to do your hair and your makeup. Then your dress will have to be fitted quickly. I imagine it will be close enough. Still, your figure has changed a bit since the last time I saw it completely uncovered. I did my best to guess."

"I…that all sounds a little excessive."

"Not at all. Your face is going to be on magazines around the world. On the front page of newspapers everywhere."

Her lips twitched. "Okay. I suppose I can submit to having a little bit of assistance."

"What's that?" he asked in mock surprise. "Is Bailey Harper actually submitting?"

"To my vanity. Not to you. Don't get used to it."

"I will see you in two hours. And I expect for you to look like a princess."

Bailey had spent the past few hours being waxed, styled, plucked and polished until she glowed. And when she looked in the mirror, she couldn't help but marvel at the incredible work a professional could do.

She had only ever had her makeup done for her once. And that was when she was in high school, and she'd decided to check out one of those makeup counters in a department store. She had come out of that experience looking like a 1980s reject, with far too much blue eye shadow and a generous helping of glitter.

This was an entirely different experience. She could hardly recognize the woman staring back at her. Her eyes were large, smoky, the charcoal gray of the shadow emphasizing her blue eyes. Her lips were painted a lovely pink color, dark and matte, very subtle.

Somehow, they had managed to style her hair into a smooth, sleek bun, the likes of which she never would have been able to manage on her own.

And the gown…it was beyond anything she had ever imagined wearing. A light shade of pink entirely covered with some sort of netting. And sewn into it were thousands of little glass beads, concentrated around the middle and dispersing over the bodice and the skirt.

With her every movement, she sparkled.

Even she could almost believe this. Even she could almost believe that she was a princess.

The dream, the fantasy hovered at the edges of her consciousness, made her soul feel like it might grow wings and fly. Or might be crushed once and for all if it went wrong.

You're nothing but a weight. You've held me down for sixteen years, Bailey. Don't think I'll spend one day missing you.

Her mother's words rang in her ears, quick to dull some of the brightness of the moment.

Whatever. She was a princess. How much of a weight could she be?

"Look at me now," she said.

She wasn't sure what she thought about all of it, not in the grand scheme of things, but in this moment, she felt pretty good.

There was a heavy knock on her bedroom door, and she assumed it was another servant, come to add another layer of makeup or perhaps to take her to meet Raphael.

"Come in," she said, not looking away from her reflection in the mirror.

The door opened, and she looked up, meeting Raphael's dark gaze as he entered the room. Her heart was thrown forward, slamming hard into the front of her chest.

"You are ready," he said.

She kept her eyes on his in the mirror, the fact it was a reflection acting as a slight buffer. "Yes. Your team of experts is in fact quite expert."

She saw a lick of fire in his eyes. "They are indeed."

"I thought we were going to meet somewhere."

"We are. Here."

She didn't want him in here. She didn't want him

looking at her like that, not with the bed so close by. She didn't want to acknowledge her own weakness.

"Well, here we are," she said, looking everywhere but at him.

"You're missing the most important part of what you'll need today," he said, stepping toward her.

She whirled around, gripping the edge of the vanity. "What's that?" she asked. "Your royal visage?"

"Not quite." He reached into the interior pocket of his jacket and pulled out a little black box.

She was pretty sure her heart stopped completely. "What are you doing?"

He opened the box, revealing a square-cut diamond on a thin band that was also encrusted with stones. Beneath it was another band, glittering yet brighter. She didn't think she had ever seen something so valuable this close. All she could think of was how much money it represented. How many months of rent it could've paid. How many months of groceries and electricity it could have provided.

It was impossible to think differently. When she had gone through life as she had.

"These are for you. Of course, just the engagement ring for now." He took hold of it, grasping it between his thumb and forefinger and holding it out to her.

And suddenly, it wasn't the value that concerned her. Her heart felt like it was shriveling, like everything was being squeezed from it. She had imagined this. Raphael proposing. Before she knew.

The ring she'd pictured had been nothing like this, and the setting had been something entirely different. She had thought he might do it that night in Vail. Out on the snowy streets, or even in his hotel room. When they were both still naked, flushed with passion.

She had fantasized about him getting down on one knee. Looking up at her, telling her she was beautiful. That he loved her. That he couldn't live without her.

Here she was, in a castle, wearing the most beautiful dress imaginable, being offered the most incredible ring. And it paled in comparison to that small, dark fantasy she'd had of him kneeling before her wearing nothing but the naked longing he felt for her on his face.

He was a different man here. There was nothing human or vulnerable about him. Nothing real. His face was stone. As though he were already preparing to become a statue on the grounds.

He wasn't asking. And she was in no position to do anything beyond taking the ring and putting it on her finger. So that was what she did. As she slipped it onto her finger, it killed her by inches.

She looked down, not quite able to believe that she was looking at her own hand. That she was wearing something quite so ostentatious.

"You do not seem pleased, Bailey. Is the ring not large enough for your taste?"

She tried to formulate a response, but the words stuck in her throat. How did she tell him that she had never imagined getting engaged, until she had met him? And then she had imagined it endlessly. And that this, though it was so much more spectacular than that initial fantasy, was nothing more than a pale imitation?

She hadn't imagined the ring.

She had imagined how full her chest would feel. How happy she would be to move forward in her life with someone by her side. To have the kind of relationship she had never dreamed she would.

Well, this was something she hadn't imagined, but she didn't feel full. She felt drained. Missing someone who had never really existed. Suddenly, she resented the man in front of her. It was easy to think he had stolen her lover from her. That they were two different people.

"You think the size of the ring is the problem?" she finally asked.

"You look upset."

"Because. Because this should have been the most romantic moment of my life. But this is all for show. There's no romance in it. There's no feeling. Just a diamond."

"A diamond would be enough for most women. And if it were not, the title of princess would supplement."

"I never dreamed of any of these things." She had never dreamed of love, either. Not before him. Dreaming was dangerous. Devastating in ways she hadn't fully realized until she'd seen those same dreams ground into ash.

"Does not every woman dream she perhaps might be a secret princess?"

"No. Sometimes a woman just dreams that she will be able to escape instability. Get an education, work for a better life. I was never afraid of that. But I was afraid of destroying my hard work. I was afraid of losing my head with a man and ending up in the exact same position as my mother. And so I did." Her voice broke on that last word, and she despised herself. For being so vulnerable with him. For giving him any more information about herself. She had been in a whole relationship all by herself back in Vail. She could see that now.

She had told him so much about who she was, what she wanted. And he had given her nothing in return. He was so skilled at keeping things focused on her, of making small talk that filled the hours but never became personal.

In combination with the physical intimacy, it had been so easy to believe that they were close. But she had never known him. And he had never intended to allow her to.

"You keep saying that. You keep comparing yourself to her. But you are here." He swept his hand across his body, indicating the space they were standing in. "As am I. I fail to see how your situation equates with hers."

"Because," she said, feeling like she was on the verge of screaming herself raw. "If you weren't a prince, if your fiancée hadn't broken up with you, I would be her. It's only your obligation and your money that separates us."

"But you have it. And you have me."

"As though that solves all of my problems without creating more."

"Yes. Terrible problems. Such as which car will you take out shopping today, which of the many forks on the table will you use to eat the delicacy laid out before you, and how on earth will you become accustomed to referring to yourself as princess?"

"Those are things," she said. "That's all."

"It is everything. As you said, you dreamed of a better life. This is a better life."

"I would have been happy with a house in the suburbs and a husband who wasn't too arrogant to function."

"I function just fine, Bailey. As you know. Though perhaps I need to refresh your memory?"

She pressed herself flat against the vanity, trying to put some distance between them while he advanced on her. Her heart was hammering a steady rhythm, so loud she was sure he could hear it. She didn't know what she wanted.

She hated that most of all.

The certainty that she shouldn't. The certainty she wished she could. Jumbling together to create a complex tangle of need inside her.

She needed him to touch her.

She needed him to stay away.

He moved to her, extending his hand and tracing her features with the tips of his fingers. She couldn't breathe. She couldn't think.

She just wanted.

"Regrettably," he said, dropping his hand back to his side, "I will have to remind you later. It is time to introduce my people to their new princess."

CHAPTER SIX

BAILEY FOUND HERSELF being ushered down a corridor of the palace at high speed. Raphael was holding tightly on to her arm as they made their way to what she presumed was the clichéd balcony they had discussed earlier.

Heels clicking loudly on the marble, an aide of some kind ran up to Raphael, her cheeks flushed, her expression tense. She handed him a piece of paper, offering no explanation. Raphael didn't pause, instead, he looked at the scrap, frowning deeply. Then he shoved the paper into his pocket, speaking past her in Italian.

He didn't bother to try to clarify what had just happened. And the only words she knew in Italian were dirty, because he'd taught them to her in bed.

She did her best to keep those thoughts at bay as they kept on rushing. Then they stopped suddenly, in front of double doors with heavy brocade curtains over them.

"You will not have to speak," he whispered into her ear, his breath hot, fanning over her neck. "Just stand next to me. Smile and wave when I do. And for God's sake, Bailey, try and look poised."

And then the doors parted. She found herself being whisked out into the fresh air as quickly as she had been dragged down the corridor. The sun was stunningly bright, washing over the mountain view. It was a shocking blue, with sharp peaks and slashes of bright white snow, fading down to the crystalline lake below. It was so intense, so beautiful that it seemed more like a painting than real life.

More surreal still was the immense crowd of people who had gathered below in the courtyard. They were hushed, standing there, still, waiting to hear from their monarch. She had never seen anything like it. And she had certainly never been in front of this many people. It was like some bad dream from junior high. Except she wasn't naked. She was wearing a designer gown.

"I am aware," Raphael said, speaking in front of a microphone that amplified his deep, rich voice, "that there has been some confusion regarding my future, and the future of this country as a result. Regrettably, my engagement to Allegra Valenti came to a rather abrupt end. And, as you have already seen in a great many of the tabloids, there has been speculation on the reasons for such a thing. I cannot deny that there is some truth to those rumors."

She had no idea what rumors he was talking about. The only headline she had seen was about the dissolution of his engagement, nothing more. She thought back to the scrap of paper he'd been passed in the hall. Had he been given all of this information only a few minutes ago? She knew Raphael was smooth. But that was impressive, even for him.

"Allegra and I wanted to do the right thing, both for my country and for her future," he continued. "But it has become abundantly clear that we were wrong in our methods. Otherwise, we would not have found ourselves in the situation. It is true—Allegra is now with someone else. And I will not deny that I am, as well. It took Allegra's courage for me to see the light, but now that I have, I hope that you will trust what I am giving to you now." His voice was solemn, sincere, and Bailey found herself being drawn in. Hanging on his every word, wondering what he might say next.

"What I am sharing with you now," he continued, "is my heart. I had thought there was perhaps no place for such a thing in politics. But I have faith in my people. Bailey Harper is the choice my heart has made. She is not from a wealthy family. Not from a blue-blooded lineage. But she is going to be my princess, and I believe in time you will all grow to love her as I do."

Bailey was sure that she was dreaming. Any minute now, she was going to wake up in her bedroom back at her apartment in Colorado. Any minute.

Rather than gaining any lucidity, things only got stranger. The crowd erupted below in a roar. Cheering. Cheering him and her and...well, both of them.

She'd never had so much positive affirmation in her life.

And then Raphael wrapped his arm around her waist, drawing her close.

He gripped her chin with his thumb and forefinger, pressing his nose against hers, his dark eyes blazing a trail of heat all the way down to her core.

She couldn't pull away. Not now. Not when they were putting on a show for the country. So, she simply had to stand there, held captive as the crowd was below. Knowing with every fiber of her being that all of the things he just said—all those words that had been so carefully crafted to sound sincere—were exactly that. A meticulously woven fiction designed to spin a tale that would sit well with a nation. Designed to create an impenetrable argument.

Anyone who rejected her now would seem spiteful. Shallow and petty. He had acknowledged that she was beneath him, and even though the words had been beautifully chosen, that was the thrust of all his argument.

Yes, she was lowborn. Yes, she was beneath him. Yes, he had tried to want someone more suitable.

But he had also lied. He had said she was the choice of his heart, when in reality, he had only chosen her because she carried his child in her womb.

She wasn't the choice of his heart. She had been the temporary choice of his libido, and that was not at all the same thing.

But he was looking down at her with such ferocity, such possessiveness, that it was difficult to reason all of that out. And anyway, there was nothing she could do now. She couldn't protest. Not even for an infinitesimal moment, because there were cameras everywhere, the entire world poised at the ready to find fault with her. And so she simply let her eyes flutter closed. Allowed him to lean in and press the softest of kisses to her lips. Almost like a brush of a feather.

Except there was such weight in it. Enough that she thought it might destroy her. That it might crack her irreparably. Reduce her to nothing where she stood.

They parted quickly, and then he raised his hand in a stiff, formal-looking wave. And she knew this was the part where she was supposed to imitate. So she did, feeling like she was playing a part in the theater. Trying to imitate her best approximation of the royal wave as she knew it from movies and parades.

Then, just as quickly as they had appeared, she was being whisked back behind the doors, carried away.

"That was it?" she asked.

"I don't answer questions. I give speeches. I do not give explanations for my decisions. What I decree is law."

"Wow. You really should see someone about that ego."

"It is not an affliction for me."

"It is for those around you," she countered.

"My ego prevents me from feeling overly concerned about that. As I am quite comfortable."

He was so handsome. Even when he was being ridiculous, so arrogant it was amazing she hadn't hauled off and slapped him. He was utter perfection. Those dark eyes and blade-straight nose. The sharp jaw. And his lips…the only soft thing about him where everything else was unyielding as granite.

"What was on that paper they gave you?" She asked the question mostly because she needed something to distract her from how very *Raphael* he was.

"Headlines are already set tomorrow to announce the engagement of Allegra Valenti to Cristian Acosta."

"Your ex is marrying someone else?"

"More importantly, she's pregnant with his baby. Which will also appear in tomorrow's headline. We will be lucky if your pregnancy doesn't appear either. Rumors are apparently already circulating. I didn't want to bring it into today's announcement, as I didn't want to undermine my points. But I saw no reason to sidestep the issue of Allegra being engaged."

"Oh. Well, that was quite the good off-the-cuff speech then."

"I have my moments. I know what my people want to hear."

"Well, that's…romantic."

"As you well know," he said, reaching up and loosening the knot on his tie. Her fingers itched to wrench it free completely. As she'd done so many times before. "There is little that is romantic about this. It isn't about romance. It's about doing what's right."

And just like that, desire turned to anger. "Oh, I do hope we can have that engraved on my wedding band."

"We *could*."

Such a strange, arrogant creature he was in his natural habitat. He could scarcely recognize her sarcasm. "No, thank you," she said, speaking slowly. "I have no desire to have that inscribed on my wedding band. I was messing with you."

"Messing with me?"

"Yes. Which I did often when we were together in Vail. It just seems sometimes like you don't remember."

"I think maybe I wasn't listening to you very closely back in Vail," he said. "Typically, I was blinded by the desire to have you."

Those words were like a clean, vicious stab through her chest. "I see. So the contents of my bra were a lot more interesting than the contents of my brain?"

"Talking to you never served a purpose," he responded, neatly sidestepping the question. "I always knew that our association would be temporary."

"But sex somehow made sense?"

"Most people assume that a sexual liaison will be temporary in some way. Unless you're looking at marriage, and often those end, too."

It was so simply put. So pragmatic. And really, not

wrong. It enraged her. Because she wanted to feel mortally wounded. Wanted to feel justified. Wanted how blindsided she had been to be about him, and not about her.

She sniffed. "Well, you lied to me."

"By omission."

Anger burned through the last shred of her pride. "You're so full of crap." She stamped, her gorgeous dress swirling around her legs. "You *absolutely* let me believe, and build off those assumptions I made early on. You did it so easily. Effortlessly. And I saw that reflected in the way that you made the announcement today. You're very good at saying what people need to hear."

"I would say that's a good quality in a leader."

"It matters much less than *doing* something. Than being sincere. What does it matter if your words make somebody feel warm all over when they listen to you talk, and then your actions leave them cold? In my case, *literally* out in the snow."

"Any dramatic tossing into the cold was your own doing. I didn't chuck you into a snowbank."

"Well, I collapsed in the snow." She watched his expression, neutral and shuttered. Maddeningly still. "In *distress*," she added. "I hope you're happy."

"It does not make me happy to have hurt you. But I fail to see how your unrealistic expectations were my fault."

"I think you fail to see how anything could be your fault ever," she spat.

"I am held to a different standard. As a result, I live my life by a different set of rules. Again, that is hardly my fault. I am under greater scrutiny. I carry heavier weight—there must be some perk to that."

"What perk? The feeling that the entire world is a trinket box you can reach into and rummage around, pulling out whatever you want and then casting it aside when you're finished? The idea that people are as disposable as *things*? That everything is here for you to use to your satisfaction? I think that goes a little bit beyond the benefits you could expect for being royalty."

"I see. And what benefits do *you* suppose I deserve? For bearing the weight of an entire nation and all of the people in it?"

"Dental? I don't know. But definitely not the right to lie about your identity."

"I wanted you," he said, grabbing hold of her arms and pressing her back against the wall, his movements sudden, swift, shocking.

He held her tight, his voice suddenly low, rough. Gone was the prince. Somehow she had managed, with a few words, to strip him back down to the man.

"I thought of nothing else but having you," he continued. "I was engaged to someone else. I knew that there was no future, and I took you anyway, because I could not imagine living in a world where I had seen you, and desired you, but not satisfied that desire. I am not a man who understands failure. I'm not a man who understands *no*."

"So you approached me as a child throwing a tantrum over a toy might?"

He growled, rolling his hips forward, the evidence of his arousal plainly felt, even through the layers of her gown. "I am not a child. And what I had was nothing like a tantrum."

He leaned closer to her, and she nearly melted. His smell, his touch, his heat…it was all too much. Too good. "Have you ever felt like your blood was on fire?" he rasped. "Have you ever felt like you would die if you didn't have something? When I saw you, that's what it was. Nothing but fire and need. I cannot explain it. Perhaps I acted uncivilized. Perhaps I played the role of villain in this. But I would do it again."

"Even knowing it ends here?"

He looked stricken by that. His dark eyes haunted. "I… I can still see no other option. Because the alternative is walking through life ablaze, and never having a chance to try and put it out."

He didn't know what was happening to him. He was… shaking.

And he knew with certainty it had nothing to do with facing a crowd of thousands, nothing to do with the eyes of the world being trained on him. Not in the least. That attention, that deference, was his birthright and he wore it with the ease he wore his own skin.

Only one thing had ever made him do this. Tremble like a child.

Bailey.

Always Bailey.

From the first.

It enraged and invigorated him in equal measure.

Because she was out of his reach. She had been. Always. He had carved out a moment of time when he could have her, just a moment. Swaths of time removed from Santa Firenze, spent in a town in the States, mostly in a hotel room with a woman he'd known he could only possess for a short while. And then a change in the tide had brought him back to her. Only now she had made it clear she wouldn't touch him. That he could never have her again, and had happily given rights to his body to other women. But there were no other women.

There hadn't been. Not from the moment he'd first met her.

Never in all his life had Prince Raphael DeSantis wanted anything that compromised the future of Santa Firenze. Never had he taken such an inconvenient mistress. Never before had he chosen a woman on the other side of the globe. A woman he could see for only snatches of time. Going more than a month without sex, often, because he couldn't slip away to Colorado. And because he could find no excitement in himself for anyone else.

The entire point of a mistress was to bring pleasure. It was the meaning of their existence.

He had certainly found pleasure in Bailey's arms, but there had been a cost. She didn't conform to his schedule, his map or his station in life. He'd had to bend to accommodate her.

He'd had her…countless times over days that were easily counted. And still, she made him shake.

Still, she treated him as if she was above this. As if she could turn away from their attraction so easily while he could not.

"I am on fire," he said, the words strong, hard. "And there you stand like ice."

"You doused the fire, Raphael. It's a bit late to regret it."

"More insipid jokes about me throwing you into the snow?"

"That's not a joke," she said. "A part of me *died* that

night. A part of me that believed in something other than my own grit for the first time in…ever. I believed in you. I believed in us. And you took it from me. You're a liar. You're a liar who would have abandoned me to raise a baby alone if not for a twist of fate."

"We met by a twist of fate," he said, releasing his hold on her arms and pressing his palms against the wall, trapping her between them. "How could our reunion have ever been anything else?"

"It could have been anything. You're a man who acts like he controls the entire world, but you're going to pretend you couldn't control what happened between us?"

"If I could have controlled what happened between us, I never would have touched you."

"Rail at fate, Raphael. Not at me. Or maybe for once rail at yourself."

She moved, as though she were going to try to dodge his hold, and he pressed himself closer. Her blue eyes glittered, anger visible there. She was ready to lash out at him if he did something she didn't want. But that was fine. He was more than ready to lash out in his own way.

Quickly, he removed one hand from the wall, sliding it around to cup the back of her head. Then he pulled her forward, claiming her mouth with all the arrogance he possessed that she claimed to be so disdainful of. She was not disdainful of it. She was weak for it. Needy. And he knew it. No matter what she said. No matter how she pretended she didn't want him anymore.

She could play it like she was disgusted with him. With all of his perceived flaws, which she was more than willing to list at the drop of a hat. And yet, without them, she would not go up in flame like this.

She pressed her hands against his chest, attempting

to push him back. But he would not be moved. Instead, he closed the distance between them, pressing her head up against the wall. His hand was trapped between her head and the hard surface, crushing his bones. But he didn't care.

She wiggled, as though she were attempting to get away. Then he angled his head, sliding his tongue across hers, the movement slow, sensual. And he felt the exact moment she went limp. The exact moment she gave in to this thing that raged between them like a starving beast.

He heard footsteps behind them, sensed that household staff members were wandering this very corridor looking the other way. He didn't care. They could stare all they wanted. She was his. She was his princess. She would be his wife. She carried his child in her womb.

Mine.

That was the word. The one that he had been a slave to, driven by, that first night he'd seen her. And he saw it now for what it was. A prophecy. He possessed her now, in every way that mattered.

And this moment, this capitulation, made it clear that he would possess her body again. She would not resist. Could not. Because regardless of how she tried to act, she was as helpless as he was. She was. He was not the only one who shook.

This little creature who seemed to imagine that she was too good for this, too good for him, was shivering in his arms like a leaf in the breeze. He was not beneath her. But, soon enough, she would be beneath him.

He rocked his hips forward, pressing his hardness into her softness, glorying in the soft gasp that he sipped from her lips.

He abandoned her mouth for a moment, kissing her

neck, down to her collarbone. He could bare her breasts here in the hall. Suck her glorious pink nipples into his mouth, so sweet, like candy. He could lift her skirts, free himself from his pants and thrust himself deep inside her.

Not a single servant in his employ would report what they had seen. They were all far too discreet, and far too well taken care of to take a chance at compromising their position in the palace.

And he did not care for his own modesty. This was his palace, after all. If he wanted to have a woman against the wall, that was his prerogative. Of course, he never had. But Bailey…he needed her. He needed her like water. Like air.

And he could feel the deprivation keenly, just as he could those other things.

He raised his hand, curling his fingers around the top of her gown, tugging the bodice down, exposing one rosy peak.

She gasped, wiggling away from him. And he was so shocked that he didn't stop her. He had lost himself. Had lost his sense of time and place.

"What are you doing?" she hissed, pulling her dress back in place. "There are…people." As if to underscore her point, a staff member, dressed all in black, rushed by quickly, her head down.

"All that you see here is mine. Mine to do with as I will. The people that work here have no other purpose but to see that my will is done. If my will is to have you out in the open, I will hardly curb my behavior for the sensibilities of those who live to serve me."

"You arrogant son of a—if you aren't concerned for your servants, if you aren't concerned for your own modesty, what about mine? And even more than that, what about the fact that I said you were not to touch me?"

"You are welcome to make edicts, Bailey. That does not mean I will comply with them. I am a law unto myself. What I want, I will have."

"So you have said. But, Raphael, do you have me?" She tilted her chin up, arching one pale brow, her expression defiant. He had never had anyone look at him like that before. As though he were something beneath contempt. "No." She supplied the answer herself. "You don't."

And then she turned on her heel and stormed down the hall, leaving him standing there, aching, desperate and in a position he did not understand.

He had shown her power. He had presented her to his people. He was giving her a title. Had installed the ungrateful creature in his palace. He had aroused her body, had proven that the fire between them was not gone.

Still, she had turned him down. Still, he had failed at an objective.

He had offered her everything in his possession, and it had not brought her to heel.

Bailey Harper was an enigma. Raphael deeply disliked enigmas.

But he would have to put the mystery of Bailey on hold. A royal wedding had been planned to take place in a few weeks' time. And by God, it would.

If not by God, then by his own hand. That, at least, would not fail.

CHAPTER SEVEN

IT WAS SURPRISINGLY simple to be the bride in a royal wedding. Given that such a thing was a worldwide spectacle, Bailey supposed it would be a great deal of work. It appeared it was not a great deal of work for the stars of the show.

It was probably helpful that most of the details had been in place already. Invitations already sent out. When she had found out that an amendment had been sent, letting people know that the name of the bride had in fact changed, she had wanted to melt into the floor and die a thousand deaths, and any number of other overdramatic and fatal things.

Focusing on her humiliation at being Raphael's pregnant replacement bride was a lot easier to handle than thinking about her disgrace in the hallway a couple of weeks back.

He had…well, he had been perilously close to having her in a public space. Had been perilously close to breaking her resolve absolutely and completely.

But then, after her foot-stomping tantrum, he'd been distant. Nothing if not circumspect. Which was just weird. Because Raphael was never circumspect. He had all the subtlety of a wrecking ball.

She startled as Raphael entered the dining room, his manner purposeful, his gaze direct. "Good evening, Bailey."

"What are you doing here?"

"Is that the customary greeting we give each other nowadays? Manners really are a dying art form."

"I haven't seen you at dinner for two weeks. And here you are. To what to do I owe the pleasure?"

"We have a menu to plan."

"Isn't the menu already planned?"

"Yes. But to Allegra's specifications. She had chosen the design for the cake and the flavors. In addition to the meal that will be served to the guests. I thought you might want your own preferences considered."

"I...well..." She didn't actually. She sort of wished that none of it was up to her. That none of it had anything to do with her. She wished that he could feel impersonal. That she could feel a victim, like she was being dragged along on this crazy, luxurious journey against her will. But when he did things like this, like acting as though there would be consideration for her as a person, and not just a trinket...

Not just another weight.

It tugged at tender, recently wounded spaces inside her. Made her hope where she desperately needed hope to be dead.

"It's cake, Bailey. Do you want to help choose it, or not?"

"Sure," she said, crossing her arms and sitting back in her chair. He had a way of taking all of his nice gestures and twisting them. Making them feel like a grievance.

"Come in," he commanded.

Bailey was confused for a moment until two members of staff came in pushing two different carts carrying covered platters. It was all set in front of her and the lids were removed quickly, revealing an array of entrées, and behind them, plates filled with miniature cakes.

"I…" She could feel her eyes go wide, could feel her entire face lighting up. She couldn't disguise it. Couldn't disguise that she thought this was pretty cool.

"A tasting menu. For your enjoyment."

"And for you?"

In answer, a new staff member came in, carrying a single platter.

"Steak for me," he said.

Then, as quickly as they had come in, the staff melted back out, leaving her alone with Raphael and several beautifully colored cakes.

Honestly, she preferred the company of the cakes.

She looked at the entrées, unsure of where to begin. There was salmon, steak, chicken and some kind of vegetable mixture.

"Vegetarian option," she said, lifting her fork and poking at the eggplant. "How very inclusive of you."

"I am nothing if not generous and exceedingly modern."

She snorted. "If you say so."

"I have to. No one else will."

"That does not surprise me." She took a bite of the vegetables, shocked when rich, buttery flavor exploded over her tongue. "Okay, that's better than I thought it would be."

"I have one of the most accomplished chefs in the world at my disposal."

"Honestly, food has been slightly difficult for me. Just hasn't tasted right for the last few weeks. I'm surprised that I'm enjoying anything." She took a bite of the chicken this time, then went down the line sampling. "I don't know how I'm supposed to choose!"

"You could choose everything."

She laughed. Because it was absurd. "Okay," she said, "I choose everything."

"Done." A member of the waitstaff came back, this time with a carafe and two cups. "Decaf for you," Raphael said, pouring a mug of coffee and passing it across the table to her.

The cakes, she saw, had little labels. Lemon chiffon with raspberry filling. Chocolate with a ganache icing. Hazelnut with mascarpone.

"I can guarantee you I'm going to need to be rolled out of here when I'm finished," she said, picking up a fork and holding it poised, unsure of which delicacy to take a bite of first.

"Go ahead," he said.

She bit her lip, trying to decide where to start. Then Raphael stood, rounding the long table and striding purposefully down the other side toward her. She stopped, watching his movements. He shoved the chair out of the way, sitting on the edge of the high-gloss surface. She blinked, a wave of shock and heat coursing through her. It had been…well, it had been two weeks since she'd been this close to him.

She had begun measuring her days in terms of how long it had been since she and Raphael had first started their relationship. She always knew exactly how long it had been.

Two weeks since they had kissed. Since he had touched her.

Three and a half months since she had said goodbye to him at the hotel. Since he had been inside her.

Suddenly all of that time felt weighted. Like it was pressing down on her, making it difficult for her to breathe. She looked up, her eyes clashing with his. His lips curved upward into a slow-burn smile that scorched her through and through.

"You like chocolate," he said, sliding his fork down through the rich, dense cake. Then he held it out to her, poised in front of her lips. "You should try that first."

Her heart was pounding, the blood rushing through her veins, hot and fast. "Haven't you ever heard of saving the best for last?"

"I believe in having the best all the time." He leaned in, the intensity in his gaze touching her deeply. "Open for me."

Those words sent an echo of sensual memory through her. Of times he had spoken those words when she was down on her knees in front of him. His voice rough, demanding. When she had wanted nothing more than to please him. And to please herself.

And, just as she had then, she parted her lips eagerly for him.

Sweet flavor burst on her tongue, dark, bitter notes following. It was like a metaphor for their entire relationship. Decadent. Intense. And something she couldn't resist, even if she should. Something she knew she shouldn't have too much of, but that she craved. All of it. Every bite.

He set the fork down, lifting up her coffee cup and handing it to her. "To cleanse your palate."

"I'm not sure coffee is a palate cleanser," she said, taking a sip anyway, her fingers brushing against his as she took the cup.

Lightning streaked through her. Would she ever be able to touch him and feel nothing? Would his skin ever just be skin? Or would it always be gasoline against her lit match?

He slid the fork through the lemon and raspberry. "Now, I think this is good, too. And it reminds me of you."

"Why is that?"

"Because," he said, bringing the fork to her mouth again. "It's tart."

He slipped the cake between her lips. "Did you just call me a tart?" she asked after she'd swallowed the bite.

"No. You aren't a tart. You are *tart*. You don't let me get away with anything. There is nothing I have done that you won't force me to answer for, is there?"

"Do you think you should be allowed to get away with not answering for your actions?"

"Yes, damn it," he said, humor playing with the edges of his mouth. "No one has ever expected me to be responsible for my actions."

"What kind of childhood must you have had?"

"One filled with everything I could have ever wanted. My needs were anticipated before even I knew them. I had a dedicated staff all to myself from the moment I came home from the hospital. Actually, I had a dedicated staff at the hospital. To hear tell of it, the entire floor was reserved for my mother when she gave birth."

"That's an extravagant beginning."

"I have never been anything but extravagant from the moment I came into this world."

"Did your dad hold you out over the balcony like *The Lion King*? Or maybe like Michael Jackson."

"I was presented to the nation when I was three days old."

"And you were adored by all," she said.

"Of course." His grin took on a decidedly arrogant tilt. "Though it was not all parties and presentations. I had to learn to be strong. For the kingdom. I could not be indulged. However, we are both indulging now. Try the next one." This time, he cut a slice off the cake, then picked it up between his thumb and forefinger. His fingertips brushed her lips. "Open for me," he said, his voice getting deeper, huskier.

She did, and he slipped his fingers and the cake into her mouth, retreating slowly, the salty flavor of his skin lingering. Arousal shot through her, need. Memory.

She couldn't really concentrate on the cake. Everything in her had zeroed in on him. On her desire for him. On this moment they were in. This little bit of connection that made her feel like maybe she did know him. Or, at least, that maybe she could. It was difficult to remember why she was so angry with him. Here, in the silence of the dining room, with the night sky beyond the window clear and bright with stars.

The two of them at this massive banquet table, with a private feast. It felt much more like fantasy than reality. These past weeks had, but this was something more. Something different. Not like some overblown princess fantasy, but something intimate. Something real.

It made her feel like she was cracking apart inside. On the verge of giving in to something she had sworn she wouldn't. But he was right there, and so warm and so very much what she really wanted.

And he was trying to make this work for her. Having her taste the food, having her sample cake. Trying to make this a little bit about her, instead of just an amendment to the wedding invitations. Almost as if he understood how she felt. As if he cared.

"There," he said, his eyes molten. He lifted his hand, dragging his thumb slowly across her cheek. "I think I have proven that I am not the selfish beast you think I am."

Something about those words sliced through the haze she was lost in. "You knew that this would…make you look like you cared."

"Of course."

"This is part of your plan. It's a thing you're doing to try and make me like you. Try and make me think you care."

"I thought of it. I thought you might care what kind of food and cake you had at the wedding."

"That's not the same as caring about me having something that I wanted."

"Yes, it is."

"No, it isn't," she insisted.

"Perhaps we are experiencing something of a language barrier. I knew you would care—therefore, I set out to do this for you. I fail to see how that proves my overwhelming selfishness."

"Did you do it because it would mean something to me, and that mattered to you? Or did you do it because you knew it would manipulate me?"

"If the result is the same, does it matter?"

"Of course it matters!" She pushed down on the table, launching herself into a standing position. "It isn't enough for you to simply know how to pull my strings. In fact, it's abhorrent."

He laughed, a hard, mocking sound. "Yes, how dare I? What a monster I am. I have brought you into my home, given you an entirely new wardrobe and presented you with a feast of cake. Truly, the abuses you suffer are beyond what anyone should be expected to endure."

"I can't be a game to you for the rest of my life. Some little puzzle that you're trying to work out constantly, and if you can make all the pieces fit, maybe you'll get me back in your bed."

He frowned. "I don't understand you," he said, frustration wearing through his aristocratic tone.

"You don't care. That's the problem. You're playing with me as if I'm a toy, and it is completely different than giving something to me because it came from a desire to please me. You only cared about what it would make me do, not what it would make me feel."

"That isn't true," he said. "I cared about what it would make you feel."

"Because if I felt good, you thought it might make me fall in line." He said nothing, his square jaw set as though it were stone. "That's what I thought."

"Why do you insist on being impossible?"

"I don't know. Why do you insist on being a liar? Why do you insist on being a prince? Why do you insist on being nothing like you were supposed to be?" She turned away from him, beginning to storm out of the room. He grabbed hold of her arm and pulled her back.

"I'm sorry there are no snowbanks outside. Nothing to fling yourself into dramatically. Perhaps you could stay here and talk to me like an adult instead of storming off like a little girl."

"I'm not a little girl," she said, consciously echoing words he had spoken to her, "as you well know."

"You do throw a very convincing tantrum."

"It's the only control I have," she launched back.

"You have me parading around the palace, putting together tasting menus and miniature cakes. Is that not control, Bailey? You have me jumping through hoops to try and gain something other than a sour expression from you. And you claim you have no control?"

"What does it cost you?"

He said nothing to that, his dark eyes inscrutable.

"Exactly," she said, turning away again.

"I don't understand the point you're trying to make," he said finally, when she was halfway between him and the door.

She turned. "You act like you're so aggrieved because you had to do something considerate for me. Something that was going to benefit you anyway. But your kitchen staff prepared the food—all you had to do was ask. You didn't give me anything at cost to yourself. It was all in service of yourself."

"If all that will ever matter to you is my reasoning behind my actions, and not my actions themselves, then we will never reach any kind of accord. I don't see what my motives matter."

"My mother kept me alive, but she let me know every day what a hardship it was. Do you think that didn't matter?"

"Of course it did," he said, his tone clipped. "But I have a responsibility. I am who I am."

"A stone?"

"Maybe so," he said, his voice hard. "But that is what withstands. It is what a nation needs. It is what our child needs. If you're going to flail around dictated by your emotions, one of us has to be firm. I am built to withstand storms, anything that might befall my country. I have to be willing to do my duty at all costs. I must be willing to sacrifice. If I am hard, it is only because it is an essential quality in a leader. I am everything I am supposed to be. I will not apologize to you."

"Good. I wouldn't want it anyway. Because you wouldn't mean it." She turned and stalked out of the room, rage making her limbs feel weak.

Dimly, she thought she might be overreacting. But she didn't really care. She had been manipulated by him from moment one. From the first moment they had seen each other. Everything he had done was suspect now. All of the things he had said since she'd come back to the palace were building on top of one another, a boulder that lodged in her chest, blocked her throat and made it impossible to breathe.

She was unsuitable. Beneath him.

You make him feel like he's on fire.

That traitorous thought glowed in her chest like an ember. Refusing to be doused. It would have to be. It just had to be. She had to get some control where he was concerned, so she wasn't continually taken in by his machinations.

She had two weeks. And then she would be his wife. It all felt so permanent. So final. Yes, there was always divorce, but she doubted it would be easy in her current position.

She was already bound to him. He wasn't just going to let her escape. She wandered over to the end of the corridor, looking out the window, over the view below. The scenery here was so beautiful, crisp and vast. It gave her the sense that she might be able to melt into it. But she couldn't. He had an army, and she had nothing. She didn't even have a passport. They wouldn't let her back into her own country.

Her throat closed tight, a sudden feeling of helplessness overwhelming her. She was marching toward this wedding day, whether she wanted to or not.

She was already in shackles. It was just that once this was over, she would be a princess in chains, rather than a commoner.

She supposed that was as good as it was going to get.

CHAPTER EIGHT

THE DAY OF the wedding dawned bright and clear, and Bailey felt it made something of a mockery out of just how stressful all of it was.

Of how much she wanted to escape into the mountains, regardless of the fact that she was pregnant, and starting to show in a completely undeniable way, in spite of the fact that there was no escape from the long arm of Raphael. Logistics were beginning to matter less and less. There was only a sense of gnawing desperation.

The only thing she could really do was try to keep her head together. Try to remember exactly what this was. It was an agreement the two of them were entering into. She would have to find a place, of course. She wasn't going to be his wife, not really. She was determined on that score. She had pride. And she had a heart to protect.

But she also wouldn't be able to sit around being idle. Motherhood would certainly take up a good portion of her time. But she wondered if there were any other things she could busy herself with.

She was in the process of getting a business degree, because she had thought it was a nice all-encompassing goal. That way, she would have the opportunity to work in a lot of different environments, and ideally start a company of her own. She had no idea what a princess might do with a business degree. Sort of moot, since at the moment, she couldn't see herself finishing it.

She had been consumed since the moment she had gotten to the palace, and studying had been low on her list of priorities. As had figuring out how to make up classes. She was in survival mode. Midterms had no place in that.

Someday, maybe. But not now. As much attention as had been paid to her appearance the day she was presented to the country, the preparation for the wedding was even more intense. She had been given some sort of scrub that was supposed to make her glow, and indeed it did.

Then she'd been made up, her hair expertly arranged, a work of architectural brilliance, and her wedding gown given a final fitting, to ensure that it flowed over her stomach so as not to draw too much attention to her expanding figure.

The announcement about the baby would wait until after the wedding, and she definitely understood why. There would be no hiding the fact that she had been pregnant prior to their marriage, but she had a feeling that once everything was settled, it would all be accepted with a bit more equanimity.

The fait accompli was definitely one of Raphael's preferred methods of operation.

In fact, it was his exclusive method of operation. If he had ever given her a choice in anything, she couldn't remember.

Liar.

She thought back to that first night. That night they

had met and he had kissed her. When passion had nearly carried her away and into his bed only a couple of hours after their first meeting. And she had told him the truth. That she was nothing more than a nervous virgin.

He had given her a choice then. He hadn't pressured her at all.

But he had seemed so different then. Yes, he had still had notes of the same arrogance she saw now. And, yes, he had definitely still liked getting his way. But it hadn't been quite so hard, or so heavy-handed.

She looked around her bedroom while the women who had been hired to prepare her for the big day continued to fuss with her hair, adding little bits of flowers to her curls and adding to the bouquet she held in her hands at the same time.

But of course, in Colorado, he hadn't been the prince of anything. Well, of course he had been, but it had been different. All of this was under his domain, which he was always the first person to remind her of. It was only just now that she realized the enormity of that.

It was about more than just a palace. It was about all the generations that had lived in it. His entire line that had ruled this country for…she didn't know for certain how many years, but she was certain that he did. Was sure that it was written on his heart. Because for all that he was insufferable, and in general kind of a beast, she had no doubt that he would bleed for his country.

As one of the women assisting her settled a necklace over her collarbone, clasping it, the weight suddenly felt excruciating. So heavy on her chest it was almost like it was suffocating her.

Bailey Harper, originally of Nebraska, was stepping into this legacy that wasn't meant for someone like her.

And he was well aware of that. He was carrying extra weight because of it.

His family tree went back hundreds of years. Hers stopped at a garage somewhere in the middle of nowhere where her mother had hooked up with a random guy.

It made her feel small. Rootless. Adrift.

Suddenly, she felt completely unequal to the task. And it had nothing to do with being his wife, or sharing his bed, which she was still determined not to do. But everything to do with the fact that she was being set up as a symbol for this country. This country that she didn't even know anything about. She hadn't even known it existed until last month.

She could see why he had chosen someone else. Why he had attempted to leave their relationship back in Colorado, where at least it made some sense.

She took a deep breath, trying to steady herself. And then the door to the bedroom opened.

"Are you ready, Princess?" It was one of Raphael's closest aides. And it was the first time he had called her princess.

She wasn't ready. She didn't think she ever would be. But it was happening all the same.

"Yes." She swallowed hard. "Yes, I'm ready."

The crowd overflowed the massive old church, just as expected. Thousands of people were in attendance, ready to see the Crown Prince of Santa Firenze finally claim his princess.

Raphael stood at the head of the altar, surveying the traditional surroundings. In this church, generations of his family had married. Generations of political alliances had been struck. That was what his marriage to Allegra was supposed to be. A marriage for his political gain. To gain the ally status of one of Italy's oldest families. It was always best to be on friendly terms with a close neighbor, and he had intended to make inroads via his wife.

Now here he stood, poised to become the first person in his family to marry for a reason other than politics. Perhaps Bailey was right. Perhaps there had been other illegitimate children, swept under the rug and cast aside. But every single marriage in the history books of the DeSantis family had been one of political importance.

Except for this. Except for him.

Raphael wondered what his father would say about such a thing if he were still alive. Would he be disappointed?

He shoved that thought off to the side. His father would have understood that this was the most expedient thing to do. This was an age of transparent media, and bastards were not so easily hidden. Not when every person on earth had a platform thanks to the internet. It would have been easy for Bailey to broadcast the fact that she was pregnant with the DeSantis heir. Easy for her to make a spectacle of his family name and his country.

His father would understand this marriage. It was not a decision driven by emotion. But a decision driven by necessity. He had weighed the cost, and he had acted.

Anyway, even without Bailey his marriage to Allegra would not have gone forward.

Yes, this was purely logical.

As the back doors to the church opened, and the music changed, his heartbeat changed, as well.

She was like an angel. An angel with a mouth that was made for sin.

She took her first step into the sanctuary, and everything in him seized tight. Her dress flowed over her curves, but it was plainly obvious to him that she was pregnant. The soft chiffon gown conformed to that small bump, and her breasts were much fuller than they had been only a few months ago. But perhaps not everyone was so in tune with changes in Bailey's figure. Likely, no one else was.

But she was his. So of course he noticed. He noticed everything about her.

He had done his very best over the last couple of weeks not to notice her at all.

They had barely spoken. Had barely made eye contact when passing each other in the hall. She had seemed happy to keep it that way, and he would not be the one to break the silence. He had refused. His pride refused. He would not bend, not for this woman.

A *nation* bowed before him. He would be damned if he bowed before one petite blonde.

And yet, as she continued down the aisle toward him, there was only that one word. That one word that he always heard echoing in his mind when he looked at her. *Mine.*

And after today, she truly would be his. She would be bound to him, legally, yes, but also with vows that were as old, if not older, than the church they were standing in. She would make promises to him here, in this place where every royal baby in his family had been christened, where every royal couple had been consecrated.

He was a man of practicality. He did not believe in

mysticism. However, he felt that making vows here had to carry more weight. That there was something truly binding in the stone walls that had witnessed so many other reverent and sovereign occasions.

All of these thoughts tripped around his mind, but none of them were as loud as the word.

Mine.

She held her head high, tilting her chin up, and he could see that her eyes were glittering. That she was fighting back tears. Bailey, his Bailey, had every emotion so close to the surface. She was hotheaded. Temperamental. And so completely genuine it was difficult to feel any annoyance about it.

She had more conviction in her every word than he had in all of his body.

But his country didn't require conviction. It required a cool head and clear leadership. That was all that had ever been required of him. He fulfilled that position without equal. Still, she seemed to find fault. She always could, his Bailey. No one else ever seemed to say anything negative at all.

Everyone else worshipped him.

Her blue eyes locked with his, and he saw no worship, no deference at all. He saw a challenge. He saw a will of iron, anger that refused to be extinguished and desire that still burned bright.

He saw a woman who was most certainly an asset to his country. Strong enough to be his princess. Strong enough to rule. How had he ever thought she was not royalty? She was. Down to her core. A woman of immovable conviction. Of deep feeling and moral standing.

She would care for his country as he did. He knew

that she would. He knew beyond anything that she would give to Santa Firenze all that he did and more. If for no other reason than to try to show him up.

Such was her stubbornness.

In that moment, he treasured it. Valued it. Because he could see that it was her strength.

She had told him about the way she had worked herself through school, how she had scraped, saved and struggled for everything she had ever had.

How had he ever seen that as anything less than equal to his own standing?

When she reached him, he took her hand in his, drawing her close. And as the priest intoned the words of the service, he let it all wash over him like a wave, absorbing it all rather than hanging on every word.

When it came time for the vows, he spoke without hesitation. He was not a soft man, not a man geared toward romance. But he was a man who knew commitment. A man who kept his word. He did not give it easily, and he had not given it to her at all prior to bringing her here, but he was giving it now. And that meant it was cast in stone.

"Upon my life," he said, his every word ringing out true and clear through the sanctuary, "I will bind myself to you. Keep myself only for you. Pledge myself to you. Body and soul. Until death separates us."

Color washed over her face as he said the words, and they resonated deep inside of him, ringing with a truth he could not deny. There was no question then of whether or not she would be his wife in body, in soul. He had spoken the words, and so they were.

For his part, he could never touch another woman, ever again. It had been so from the moment he had seen her. As deeply imprinted in his soul as that sure and knowing possessiveness that had gripped him from the first moment he'd laid eyes on her.

Mine.

And he was hers, and no one else's.

She repeated his same words back to him, her voice muted, her eyes downcast. And he could see that that same certainty that he felt, down to his very soul, was not shared by her.

It could not be so. She was *his*. His and no one else's. He had bound himself to her. And he had meant his every vow. He would keep it. He would keep every one.

And then it was announced that he could kiss his bride.

He wrapped his arm around her waist, pulling her close, gripping her chin as he brought his face down to hers, and kissed her like it was a brand. As though he were trying to burn that same mark onto her soul that he bore on his.

When they parted, her eyes were bright, her breathing swift, rapid.

He looked at her, everything in him on high alert, determined.

Then, as the crowd cheered for them, for their marriage, he leaned over, his lips brushing against her ear. "You are mine," he whispered. "And I have decided that I will have my wedding night."

It was absolutely impossible to concentrate on the wedding feast, on the chocolate cake that she had chosen and the delicious steak that she had been served earlier. Difficult to do anything but smile brutally as well-wishers filtered through, telling them how pleased they were to have her as princess.

Every voice was a dull, murky mumble. Every taste bland. Because all she could think of was that husky whispered promise he had made up at the altar. Not his public proclamation, but that carnal vow made only for her ears.

That he would have his wedding night.

She had been determined that he wouldn't. And she had been certain he had understood. After all, they had barely spoken at all for the last couple of weeks. Why would he think anything had changed?

She was…she didn't know how she felt. She didn't know what to think. Except she wished that this interminable reception would continue to be interminable. Wished that it would go on so that she didn't have to face being alone with her new husband.

Her *husband*.

She had just stood in front of a nation, in front of the world really, and made promises to this man that she would never be able to break.

She was his captive. She could see clearly enough that she had been from the moment she had first stepped onto his private plane. Perhaps from the moment she had taken his hand outside the diner and said she would, in fact, go home with him on that first night they'd met.

The marriage was just a formality.

She had fooled herself into believing that she had some kind of bargaining power. That he had seen her side of things. That perhaps he understood that things would be better if they didn't have an intimate relationship. Clearly, it had all been a ruse. Something to lull her into a false sense of security.

Or maybe to keep her from screaming at him every day for the last two weeks.

She looked over at him, her eyes catching hold of his. Her heart felt like a bird fluttering in a cage, desperate to get out. At least if her heart escaped, it might be able to fly away from this place. Away from this man who had the potential to be so devastating. If she could only keep her heart safe, then maybe the rest would be okay. She enjoyed having sex with Raphael.

She pressed her mouth into a thin line. That was such an insipid description of what being with him was. It was never about the physical. It never had been. Yes, it felt amazing. Yes, he gave her pleasure unlike anything she'd ever known. But it had never ended there. Not for her.

She had felt connected to him from the moment she'd met him. And when his body had joined with hers, she had felt like everything made sense. Like he had uncovered hidden pieces of her that made so many other things fall into place.

She could not separate that from emotion. Couldn't excise it from what she felt for him.

Whether it was anger or love, there was always something. Always something bigger than she was.

She had loved him back then. Truly. Desperately. Had been ready to spend the rest of her life with him. But then she had to face the fact that she didn't know him. Then he had broken her heart. Then he had swept her off to a castle and shown her demonstrations of power the likes of which she had never seen before.

She had loved the man he was. She didn't know how she felt about this man. This man she had just married. This man who was, sadly, the reality of her fantasy lover, who she'd had over long weekends every couple of months.

She felt silly just then. That she had managed to create such intense feelings for someone that she really hadn't spent all that much time with. That she had allowed herself to fall in love with a man who was so clearly a work of fiction. And that she was now bound to his true self, someone who would never love her. Someone who would only take.

They continued to make their way through the reception, managing to speak to just about everyone but each other.

And then came the time for their grand exit. It was very traditional, with rice thrown as they walked out of the elegant reception hall. She tried to smile. Tried to look like a new bride should. But she found she could not. It was far too difficult. Not when she felt like she was made of lead.

They made their way outside. It was cold and crisp, the night air like a baptism, washing away the events of the day.

But only for a moment.

He led her to the palace, up the steps and in through the massive doors.

They stopped in the entryway, and he regarded her closely. "This is your home now," he said. "Truly. It is a part of you."

She looked around, her pulse throbbing a steady rhythm at the base of her throat. "And to think, my biggest aspiration was perhaps to one day own a house in a nice neighborhood."

"Well, look at it this way. You won't have to deal with a homeowner's association here."

"Just legions of staff and a husband who thinks he rules the world."

"Only a country," he responded. The heat in his dark eyes grew more intense, and he lowered his head, his face a breath away from hers. "Let's go to bed."

"I told you. I told you that I was not…that we were not…"

Something changed in his expression then. He was still perfectly pressed. Still dressed in that meticulously tailored tuxedo he had worn to the wedding. His hair was perfectly styled, not a bit of it out of place.

But it was like a switch had been thrown, and every last vestige of civility was gone from his face.

He was wild just then. Feral.

A predator who had most definitely set his sights on her.

"I know what you said," he responded. "But I made vows to you before my country. Before my ancestors. And I, for my part, intend to keep them. You may not wish to have me as your husband, but I am going to make you my wife."

And then he swept her up into his arms, holding her against his hard chest. She was too shocked to protest. He propelled them both toward the stairs, toward his room.

She knew then that the decision had been made. That, as with all things, once Raphael had set his mind to something, he would not be deterred.

She held on to him, because, after all, she didn't want him to drop her. Held on to him until he brought them both to his chamber, a set of rooms that she had not been in before. He carried her over the threshold, as though he were any groom on his wedding night.

He turned and shut the doors, the sound one of absolute finality.

Then he faced her, his expression all lean hunger.

"And now, my wife," he said, taking a step toward her, "you will be mine."

CHAPTER NINE

BAILEY SEARCHED HIS face, looking for a hint of calculation. Searching for an indication that this was part of his plan.

But there was nothing. That cool sophistication was gone. Burned away. He wasn't the man she'd met in the diner back in the States, and he wasn't the prince.

He was something else entirely. Something foreign and familiar all at once.

He advanced on her, his eyes a broad spectrum of flame, burning with every dark emotion. Rage. Need.

Fear.

Of himself or her she didn't know.

It didn't really matter, either, because an answer to that wouldn't change his course. Wouldn't change what was about to happen here. She backed against the wall, letting him advance on her.

He reached out, grabbing hold of the delicate neckline of her wedding gown and tugging hard. The whisper-thin layers of fabric tore, the bodice separating at the seams, exposing the strapless, lacy bra she wore underneath.

She gasped, pressing herself more firmly against the wall.

"Is that how you look at me now?" he asked. "As though I am your enemy?" He cupped her cheek, sliding his thumb across her delicate skin. "As though you don't know me? As though I have not known your body in nearly every way possible?"

"That was different," she said, her tone stiff. "It is different. I don't know you. Not anymore. I never did. The man that I met, the man that I thought you were, doesn't exist. And I'm not going to have sex with a stranger."

"A stranger?" He chuckled, a humorless sound. Then he leaned in, pressing a kiss to her neck, his lips hot and enticing against her skin. "Would a stranger know that if he were to touch you here," he said, sliding his hand down to cup her breast, his thumb resting beneath the lower curve, "that you will start trembling?"

Her traitorous body did exactly that. Shaking beneath his touch, a quivering, needy thing. She was every inch his creature, and he knew it. The bastard knew it.

"Would a stranger know," he said, "that if he were to taste you like this—" he slid his tongue down the side of her neck "—that you will go up in flames?"

She did. Just like that, she did.

"Trust isn't the same thing," she said, panting. She was ashamed that she was so transparent, but she didn't know if there was anything for it.

"I don't care about your trust, *amore mia*. I care about this." He kissed the edge of her mouth, and a lightning bolt shot through her.

She turned her head to the side, closing her eyes tight. "No," she said.

He growled, gripping her arms and looking into her eyes. "What will it take? What do I have to do? I have already lowered myself to admit to you that you make me burn. That I have not been the same since the moment that I saw you in that diner. I have confessed these things to you, and it is not enough. What will it take?" he ground out.

"N-nothing," she said, the lie tasting bitter on her lips. "There's nothing you can do."

"Do you want me to beg?" he asked, the words hard, full of disdain. "Is that what you want? My waitress wife, do you suppose that you are worthy of me lowering myself for you?"

"I suppose that I deserve nothing less than absolute contrition from the man who abandoned me when I was pregnant with his child. The man who would never know that he was having a baby were it not for a freak change of circumstances." And that was not a lie.

"Contrition doesn't come for free." His black eyes glittered like obsidian. Hard. Sharp. "Perhaps you should remind me of what I enjoyed about you in the first place. Because at the moment, I am having a difficult time remembering."

"Or, perhaps," she said, "you can go to your room and find comfort with your right hand. I am not a thing that you can use. I am a woman. You cannot treat me like something you can simply retrieve at will, then toss back when you're finished."

He dropped to his knees in front of her, curling his fingers around the material of the gown as he went, dragging it down into a pool of ruined material on the floor. "Begging is what you require then?"

Her breath hitched. "I didn't say that."

"You would have me beg to be with my own wife. Then so be it." He looked up at her, his expression hard, and then he grabbed hold of the waistband of her white lace panties, tugging them to her knees. "Consider this my supplication."

"Raphael—"

Whatever she had been about to say was lost as his strong, firm hands grabbed hold of her hips, steadying her. Then, he leaned in, inhaling deeply, pressing his face against the tender skin of her inner thigh. "I have dreamed of this," he rasped. "I have dreamed of you."

He moved to her center, sliding his tongue over wet, needy flesh, tasting her deeply. She shivered, pleasure cutting into her like a knife. She reached out, grabbing hold of his shoulder, curling her fingers around his jacket, clinging to him.

Was she so weak?

As he moved even more deeply, his tongue created a wicked kind of magic that moved through her body like a dark enchantment.

She wanted to cry. Because of how good it felt. Because of how weak she felt. Because she was failing herself. But she realized she wanted to have him force this seduction on her. She wanted to submit to it. To tell herself that she was unwilling. That all the power was with him, so that she could absolve herself of any sin. Of any guilt.

You want it. You want him.

She squeezed her eyes shut, letting go of him. But she didn't move away from him. She raised her arms up over her head, pressing her knuckles firmly into the wall, as though she were releasing her culpability in this.

Her heart beat a steady rhythm, each and every pulse calling her a liar. As Raphael continued to push her higher, further, faster. He was ruthless in his exploration of her, his tongue and fingers seeking out each delightful point of pleasure.

He dragged his fingers through her slick folds, pressed a finger deep inside her as he continued the wicked assault with his tongue.

She hadn't allowed herself pleasure since he had left her. It had been punishment for her stupidity, and then, when she had come here to the palace, something she refused to allow herself because she would only be imagining Raphael.

She was strung so tight she was certain that it would take very little to snap her in two.

He knew it, too. He could feel how wet she was for him, how needy. She knew that he could feel her now, her internal muscles tightening around him as he continued to pleasure her. He knew how close she was to the edge.

That bit of humiliation should have pulled her back. Instead, it spurred her on. Brought her arousal up to impossible heights.

"Raphael," she gasped. "Raphael… I can't."

"You can," he said, his breath hot on the source of her pleasure. "And you will. Come for me, Bailey."

The command was as arrogant as any he'd ever issued. As though he, and he alone, had dominion over her body. As though she were powerless to resist any command he might issue, even one such as this.

He was right.

The words pushed her over the edge, sending her hurtling down toward the very bottom of an abyss. And when she hit, she shattered. She became a thousand sparkling pieces, shimmering with pleasure, with the glorious release that made her feel weightless, free. For the first time since her life had been broken apart and glued back together, badly, she felt free.

She felt like herself.

As though he had not just given her a physical release but had released a part of her she had ruthlessly squashed, shamed, left for dead.

She inhaled sharply, and then, suddenly, he was in front of her again, claiming her mouth with his, the taste of her desire on his lips. Carnal. Wild.

He swept her back into his arms, carrying her across the room and depositing her on the bed. Her heart tripped over itself as she watched those deft, blunt fingers working the buttons on his shirt, wrenching his tie free, casting the last vestiges of civility down to the floor.

She drank in the sight of him, hunger roaring through her, as though she had not just found release.

The dim light cast his muscles into sharp relief, the dips and hollows of his abs exaggerated in the glow cast over him by the one lamp that was lit. She was breathless. Caught up in her desire. Just as she had been from the beginning.

There was no thought of consequences. No deference paid to self-preservation. What was the point? She might live a life preserved, but she wouldn't be herself. She would be squished and hidden. Safe but unused. Like a book that had never been read.

She watched, transfixed, as he worked his belt through the buckle, slid it slowly through the loops on his pants. She looked up, looked into his eyes. They burned her, straight down to her center, down to her soul. It wasn't enough that he had complete and total reign over her body, he seemed to demand it in every other capacity, as well.

Nothing more could be expected of Raphael, not really.

His arrogance knew no boundaries—why should it find any here?

She let her eyes drop again, and this time she was held transfixed by the outline of his erection, the absolute evidence of his desire for her. That he was just as weak, just as mortal as she was right now.

It had been so easy to remember the control this yawning, needy thing had exerted over her that she had forgotten about the power she held over him. How had that happened? Hadn't he demonstrated it when he'd fallen to his knees in front of her?

He had shown her, at every turn, that she held sway over him, and yet she had focused on the needy sense of powerlessness inside herself.

Something inside her turned, like a key in a lock, and she felt as though she was seeing all of this differently now. As though a revelation had tumbled down upon her, and she couldn't go back to viewing it quite as she had before.

She rose up onto her knees, reaching behind her and undoing the four little hooks that held her bra in place. She threw the insubstantial confection down to the floor, kneeling there before him, completely naked now. She refused to hide, refused to cower.

Refused to feel ashamed.

That had nothing to do with Raphael, or anything he had ever made her feel. But with herself. She had been bound up in this idea of failure. That desiring Raphael, that desiring anyone, had led her to her doom. That it made her lesser.

But all of that was her baggage. Bound up in cracked pride, because she had always been just a little bit disdainful of her mother and her actions. But it was only pride. Pride that kept her bound and lonely, that would never keep her warm at night, that would never bring her any sense of fulfillment. And maybe Raphael wouldn't either. Maybe this was simply the road to fresh heartbreak.

But she wanted him. And he wanted her back.

It was enough for now. For this moment.

"You made me wait too long," he said, his voice rough.

He shoved his pants down his lean hips, uncovering his body. Her breath rushed from her lungs. It had been way too long since she had seen him naked. Of course, images of him were burned into her brain, fantasies that wouldn't leave her alone even when she desperately needed them to.

But it wasn't the same. Wasn't the same as being so close to him she could touch him. Could taste him.

She moved to the edge of the bed, reaching out slowly, curling her fingers around his shoulder. Then she bent down, kissing his chest lightly. His muscle jumped beneath her lips, his entire body jerking backward, as though he had been burned.

Oh, yes, she had power here.

She nibbled her way up to his jaw, traced that square angle down to his chin with the tip of her tongue, then worked her way up to his lips, sliding her tongue between them, tasting him in a way that mimicked what he had done between her thighs only a few moments ago.

He wrapped his arm around her waist, growling, pushing her down onto the bed, onto her back. He kissed her deeply, taking absolutely no quarter, employing no gentleness at all. But that was fine. That wasn't what she needed. She needed him out of control, as he had been from the moment they had first come into this bedroom. That realization made something bloom, hot and hopeful, in her chest.

This wasn't calculated. This was nothing like their cake tasting two weeks ago. He wasn't doing this to manipulate. He was doing it because he had no other choice. Because he was at the end of his control.

Satisfaction pooled hot and low in her stomach, arousal wrenching itself tighter inside her. His hardness was settled between her legs, sliding against where she was already beginning to feel needy for him again. But an orgasm alone wouldn't be enough this time. She needed to be filled by him. Needed him inside her.

The words hovered on the edge of her lips, but she felt like they might cost her something much dearer than she was willing to pay. There wasn't room for that.

"I want you," she said. "I want you inside of me."

He groaned, the sound a prayer and a curse all at once. Then the blunt head of his arousal pressed up against the entrance to her body, and he tested her, slowly, taking all the care he had taken with her the first time.

Tears stung her eyes. She didn't want tenderness. She wanted fierce, hot and fast. She wanted to satisfy this growling beast inside her.

She braced her hands on his back, then slid them down to his rear, grabbing hold of him tightly and urging him deep inside her. She gasped as he filled her, wholly and completely, nearly to the point of pain.

She relished it. All of it.

She looked up at him, at the tension in his face, the cords of his neck standing out, evidence of the intense amount of power it was taking for him to control himself. She loved that. Seeing how profoundly she affected him. Truly realizing that she wasn't alone in this insanity.

He had lied to her. He had broken her trust.

But this was true. It was real, and it was honest. It was everything. She wasn't entirely sure she knew everything of who he was. Wasn't sure where the truth of the man she had first met ended and the reality of this prince who she'd married began.

She didn't know. She wasn't sure she ever would. But this, this meeting of their bodies, this intense, deep connection that occurred when the two of them were together, was honest. It was the same now as it had been then. He didn't feel like a stranger.

She knew him in her soul.

She knew him in this honesty. In his every touch and his every thrust as he began to move inside her. This was real. Pure and true, and the fact that she had ever felt ashamed seemed wrong now.

She exulted in it. In him. In the rightness of it. Nothing had felt right for so many months now, but this did.

She was caught up in it, in him, swept away on a tide of pleasure as release washed through her again and again. And when he shattered, when he found his own, she gloried in that, too. In his big body shuddering as he spent himself deep inside her.

When it was over, there was no sound but their frac-

tured breathing echoing off the walls, nothing but a pro-
found feeling of finality. It was no longer a question,
whether they would end up here. Because they had. No
longer a question of whether he would continue to pur-
sue, and she would continue to resist. It was done. And
now that it was, she knew there would be no going back.

And now she wondered why she had wanted to in
the first place. Raphael was the only man she had ever
wanted. It didn't matter whether she thought he was a
businessman or knew that he was a prince. It didn't matter if it was back in the United States or if it was here.

He was the thing her heart desired, more than anything. And she was justly entitled to her anger and her
heartbreak over how he had treated her. But they had
this chance. This chance to be married. To be together.
And she had been choosing to cling to anger.

Anger was a hot, destructive shield to use. And she
was beginning to realize there was a great cost to protection anyway. For the sake of pride, for the fear of
being hurt, she had been intent on keeping something
she wanted from herself.

All of it tangled up in that self-flagellation she'd been
lost in for so many months.

If she was going to live with him, raise a child with
him, be his wife, there was going to be a certain amount
of letting go involved. Of deciding to put the past behind
them. Of making where they ended up more important
than where they had begun.

She breathed in his scent, wrapped her arms around
his neck, held him close. And she let all the rest go.

CHAPTER TEN

WHEN RAPHAEL WOKE up in the morning there was a woman wrapped around him. It was notable, because it had been so long since that had happened. He opened his eyes, looking out across the broad expanse of his chamber. And he saw a wedding dress, torn into two pieces and left on the floor like a moth that had been stripped of its wings.

He remembered then. Backing Bailey against the wall. Tearing the top of her gown. Holding her tightly against his mouth while he had unleashed all the pent-up anger and need that roared through him like an untamed animal.

Yes, suddenly he remembered all of that.

He sat up, and the swift motion disturbed Bailey, who had been wound up in him in such a way it was impossible for him to take a breath without affecting her.

She opened her eyes, the foggy, sleepy blue sending a wave of longing through him that made his teeth ache. He had no idea what that meant. No idea why. She was here, and she was naked, which meant there was absolutely nothing for him to long for. He had everything.

This woman, who was now his wife, this palace and

his kingdom. There was nothing else. No reason for the hollow, bone-chilling ache that pervaded him now.

And yet it persisted.

"Good morning," she mumbled.

"Is it?" he asked, clipped.

He found himself extricating himself from her hold and getting out of bed, walking across the room, kneeling down to examine the damage he had done to the dress.

"It's a little bit late for regret," she said, sitting up, holding the sheet up over her breasts. Her cheeks were extra pink this morning, her mouth a bit swollen. He could not remember how many times he had reached for her last night, desperate to sate the desire for her that had built itself inside him to a fever pitch.

She bore the marks of that. Of his passion. Of his selfish desperation. As did the dress.

"I should have thought it was never too late for regret. In fact, you have been demonstrating that to me over the course of the past month. Just how very much you regret me. I'm beginning to think that perhaps you're not entirely crazy to feel that way."

She frowned. "Yes, well, nice to know you won't become completely crazy, now that you've married me."

"I wasn't myself last night."

"Yes, you were. You were completely yourself. You felt you were entitled to something that you weren't being given and reacted as you do."

"You said you wanted me," he said. He was thinking of that moment when she had told him, with that desperate, needy sigh on her lips, that she wanted him inside her. She had said that. She had wanted it.

"Yes, I did. I have. From the moment you came back to me, I've wanted you. That isn't the issue."

"What is?" He stood, holding the remaining pieces of the dress in his hands. "Because, for someone who claims to want me, you did an admirable job of resisting me at every turn."

"I don't want to be a salve for your wounded ego. And I don't want to be a challenge to your masculine pride. That's what I was saying. You're a man who is accustomed to having everything he wants. I don't want to be just another one of those things. I want to mean something more than that to you."

"You want to cost me something," he said, understanding filling him slowly. "That is what you said the other day. That my gesture with the cake was empty because there was no cost to me."

"You've cost me an awful lot, Raphael. I don't suppose it's extremely selfish to wish that I cost you a little something, too."

"You think you have not? I have vowed never to touch another woman."

"The bare minimum requirement for marriage, I should think."

"I am the first person in my family to marry for a reason other than political gain." Finally, finally that elicited some reaction from her. Finally that caused a change in her expression. "I broke centuries of tradition to marry you. You have no connection that could possibly benefit Santa Firenze. What I did, I did for our baby. Yes, I could have hidden you away. I could have paid you off, given you some exorbitant sum of money, but that isn't what I wanted. I wanted my child here. With me."

"And me?" she asked, her voice small.

He let the dress fall to the floor, and he crossed the space between them. He looked at her, and she turned her gaze away. He reached out, taking hold of her chin, directing her eyes back to his. "I have not been with another woman since the day I met you. When I broke things off with you, I did my very best to try and turn my focus to Allegra. She and I never had much of a connection. We hardly had anything to do with each other. She and her entire family would accompany me on various holidays, but she and I were never tempted to spend time alone. She was ideal, in other words."

"How is it ideal to not want your wife?"

"It is ideal to not find your wife a…a distraction. I hoped… I sincerely hoped that when I ended things with you I would be able to find some sort of desire in myself for her. She was going to be my wife, after all, and a life wanting someone else was unthinkable."

"And how did that go for you?" she asked, looking comically hopeful.

"The next time I saw her after you and I broke up, I purposed that I would kiss her." He cleared his throat. "A real kiss. Not just a kiss on her head. But then I saw her and… I could not. I kept seeing you. Every time I saw a woman with blond hair, I would hope that she would turn around and it would be you. I want you to distraction, Bailey. It is wholly inconvenient."

"So, I'm not a completely negligible part of this package?"

"I suppose I wasn't being entirely truthful when I said that I didn't marry for any kind of gain. When I saw you walking down the aisle toward me yesterday, I realized that your strength is only going to be an asset to me, and to this country. You may not have political connections, but I admire you. You worked very hard to get where you are in life, and I don't know very many people who can say the same."

"You work hard, Raphael."

"Undoubtedly," he responded. "But I was given all of this. That's different."

As soon as the words left his mouth, he realized how true it was. How his confidence, his power, was built on something handed down. And in order for it to be handed down effectively, his father had handed his arrogance and certainty down, as well.

He had molded him perfectly. Taught him with so many gestures that there was nothing he could not have while demonstrating at the same time there was nothing more important than the country.

"That's more impressive in some regards," Bailey said. "Seeing as when you haven't earned something often it means less. And it would be easy for you to feel less of an obligation to your country because you didn't achieve your position through hard work. So, I can easily make an argument to support the fact that you're actually pretty amazing."

"Suddenly you have kind words for me, Bailey? Please tell me you did not sustain a head injury last night."

She smiled, a rather impish expression that tugged something deep inside him. It was strange, and not entirely unpleasant, to have a moment where she wasn't at odds with him. He had told himself that it didn't matter, that the only thing that was really bothering him was the prolonged celibacy.

He had told himself that he didn't miss her companionship, just her body. That the entire relationship they'd had back in Colorado was something of a farce. A strange experiment on his end. Being with a woman who had no idea who he was, interacting with her as a typical man would.

But her smile sent such a ferocious flood of warmth through his body that it was difficult to believe that now.

He wanted to do something for her. But he couldn't think what. He had married her, after all. Made her a princess. He wasn't exactly sure what you did to top that gesture. Though, perhaps, a honeymoon.

"Have you ever been to Paris?" he asked.

"No," she said. "But I still don't have a passport."

"You are the princess of Santa Firenze. Your travel documents will be sorted by the palace." He watched her cheeks turn pink, her pleasure obvious. "You are excited about the idea of going to Paris?"

"Of course I am. Who wouldn't be? I've dreamed about seeing it, but I never thought I would. My fantasies ran toward cutting myself above the poverty line. Getting a good job. World travel never really featured."

"Well, world travel is essentially in your job description now."

"Lucky me," she said. "And I mean that. That was not sarcasm."

"No sarcasm?" he asked, with mock shock coloring his tone. "It's amazing you didn't injure yourself."

"You're giving me Paris. I felt, at the least, I owed you a little sincerity."

His chest tightened. He wasn't sure why, but he had the strange feeling of impending doom, rolling over his shoulders like a dark, heavy cloak. "I wouldn't give me too much. But I shall alert the staff of our plans, and they will pack your things."

"We're going now?"

"Paris has waited for you long enough."

CHAPTER ELEVEN

THE FIRST SIGHT of the city took Bailey's breath away. Everything was so old. She had noticed the same thing in Santa Firenze. Maybe that was a strange observation, but everything in the United States was relatively new, particularly things in the West. They didn't have this sort of history, embedded into every brick, into each and every fine scroll carved into the stonework.

The art, the history, was like a living thing, making the architecture, the very air around them, seem like so much more.

They drove along a road that bordered the Seine, the gray water reflecting the clouds above, the row of buildings, old churches and museums on the other side of them like an impenetrable sentry wall.

The penthouse that Raphael had secured for them was rich in details, from the crown molding down to the gold fixtures in the kitchen and bathroom. There was a spread of cheese and bread waiting for them upon arrival, along with a bottle of champagne that Bailey would not be availing herself of.

The master suite was brilliantly appointed, and the closet was already full. Full of beautiful garments that,

Raphael informed her, a personal shopper had chosen specifically for Bailey.

Among them was a rich, green gown made of flowing silk. Silk that would undoubtedly show her growing pregnancy.

"When am I supposed to wear this?" she asked, brushing her fingertips down the fine fabric.

"Tonight," he said, his tone nonchalant.

"I didn't know we had plans."

"There is a private dinner and art exhibition at the Musée d'Orsay tonight. I thought it was something you would probably enjoy, and I thought that the man in charge of the event would likely enjoy the attendance of royalty, even if it were last minute. I was correct. At least on that score. I hope I was correct about you, too."

His expression was so sincere, his tone hopeful. It was…it was so unusual to see Raphael looking something less than certain. But he did. Just as he had done this morning after their wedding night. He had been concerned that he had crossed a line. The fact that he was capable of such concern was encouraging.

He wasn't pulling that veil of arrogance back into place at every opportunity. At least, not today.

"Of course I want to go. A beautiful dress, wonderful food, famous art. What's not to like?"

His smile was slow, and he nodded. "Yes. You are correct."

"You were afraid that I wouldn't like a beautiful dress and a private evening at a museum?"

"I am eternally at a loss with you," he said, his frustration clear. "I had imagined that you would fall to your knees in gratitude the moment I told you I would marry you. That you would see what an honor I was bestowing upon you when you caught sight of my palace. So far, you have been distinctly unimpressed with me."

"It's not you I'm unimpressed with," she responded. "Just the things."

"I am the things," he said.

She frowned, taking a step toward him, reaching up, pressing her palm to his cheek. "How can that be? Didn't I meet you before I knew you had any of that?"

"That was different."

Her heart sank a little bit. "Yes," she said, "it was different."

It was different because it had been completely genuine on her part and a ruse on his. Different because she had imagined they would have a future, while he knew for a fact they wouldn't.

"We will leave in a couple of hours for the party."

"I might want to… I mean, I might take a walk. Just for an hour or so."

He frowned. "You can't do that."

"I'm in Paris. I would like to have a look around." And she needed just a little bit of distance to catch her breath. It was difficult to be under the influence of Raphael. He was so very much. She was trying to find that line between protecting herself and sacrificing herself.

She didn't want to wall him off, not completely, but she needed to have some defenses in place, surely.

"You are royalty. You cannot simply walk around the streets by yourself."

"You really think anyone will recognize me?"

"You are the favored headline at the moment, *cara*. I think you would be recognized within seconds."

"Then I guess I'll get ready," she said, monotone.

"What else could I possibly want to do in Paris but apply makeup?"

"How quickly the tide turns." His expression was grim. "I'm not trying to ruin your life. I'm just being realistic."

She frowned. "Okay." She let out a long, slow breath. "I'm sorry. I'm actually being a little unreasonable. I'll just get ready."

By the time she got herself beautified, it was time to go. She looked at herself in the vanity mirror, frowning. Yes, it was very apparent that she was pregnant.

"I hope you're prepared for the fact that we are essentially making an announcement tonight," she said, walking out into the main living area of the penthouse.

Raphael looked up from his newspaper, his jaw going slack. "Oh," was all he said. More of a noise than an actual response.

"What does that mean?"

He stood, closing the distance between them. He stopped just short of her, not touching her at all.

"Come on, Raphael—you have to say something, or I'm going to go back into the bedroom and change into my sweats."

"No, you will not," he said, his expression fierce. "You are perfect. A jewel come to life."

"I didn't even have a professional makeup artist tonight," she said, pressing for yet more compliments, because this one made her feel warm all over. "And," she added, reaching up to play with a strand of loose hair, "I did my hair, too."

"It suits you. Possibly because it is you. Utterly and completely."

He leaned in, kissing her forehead. It was a strange,

affectionate gesture, void of the usual carnal sexuality that was typically laced through their other kisses.

Then he angled his head and kissed her lips. This one had all the usual carnal sexuality and then some.

"We have to go," he said. "Or I will have you out of that dress, and we will never make it to the museum."

"People are going to know I'm pregnant," she prodded. "You didn't say anything about that."

"I'm proud of your pregnancy. Of the fact you are my wife, that you are carrying my child. I'm pleased to show the world."

"That was the right thing to say," she said, stretching up on her toes and kissing him.

"There's a first time for everything," he said, amusement in his voice.

Somehow they managed to make it to the museum with all of Bailey's makeup intact, which was a miracle, seeing as Raphael had done his very best to kiss most of it off in the car. The museum was beautiful, set for a dinner in one room with ornate table settings and large bouquets of lushly colored flowers.

Men in black suits and women in gowns that ran the spectrum of the rainbow milled about the room making conversation, moving through the large building, looking at the various exhibits that were open to the guests.

The hors d'oeuvres that were being served looked lovely, but Bailey found she was more interested in examining the art.

She managed to tear herself away from one of the overly enthusiastic women who had grabbed her upon entry, excited to meet a princess. And had been obviously angling to get Bailey to comment on her condition. Bailey found it all extremely strange. Being the center of any kind of attention.

Only a few short weeks ago, she'd been the wait-staff. Now she was a princess. A guest of honor. It was enough to make her head spin. And definitely enough to make her seek out a quiet moment.

She made her way to the wing of the museum that housed the sculptures. Bailey wandered through the exquisite marble figures, marveling at the expressive-ness of the features. They weren't cold, in spite of the smooth, white stone that was used to fashion them. In fact, she could almost believe that any moment they might come to life.

She paused in front of the statue of a kneeling woman, one of the rare female figures that was fully clothed.

"Here you are."

She turned to see Raphael coming toward her. Her heart clenched tight. And so did other things. Really, he looked amazing in a tux. He shouldn't wear anything else. Unless he was naked. He could be naked.

"Over relating to the plight of Joan of Arc?"

She looked down at the statue's small plaque. "I guess I was."

"Great is your martyrdom."

"Sometimes it feels like it is."

"A very brave creature you are, Bailey Harper."

"That's Princess Bailey DeSantis to you," she said, keeping her tone arch.

"My apologies for the grave error." He moved closer to her. "You're enjoying the art?"

"Yes. I've never seen anything like it. I mean, I've been to museums before, but nothing with works like this. This is…it's exquisite."

"You know, only this floor is open to guests tonight."

"I know."

"I made arrangements to get us up to one of the top floors. I thought you might like to see Manet."

She looked over at him, her heart pounding heavily. "I would… I would love that. But it isn't supposed to be open."

"I am Prince Raphael DeSantis," he said. "The rules of mere mortal men do not apply to me. Nor should they."

She laughed. She couldn't help herself. "I'm sorry— sometimes I forget I'm married to a demigod."

"You wound me so. Only a demigod?"

"I'm sorry. Jove reincarnated?"

"Much better." He extended his arm. "Shall we?"

They took an elevator until it was required they take the stairs, then made their way to a silent floor, high above the activity that was happening below. The settings were sparse, nothing but blocks of black walls dividing a large space. But that was because the show belonged to the artwork that was hanging there.

Raphael stayed silent while they wandered through the displays, while she paused at the paintings. Strangely, while standing in front of one that featured a woman at a picnic—the men were dressed, and she was naked—Bailey could suddenly relate to that woman. Uncovered like that for all to see while her companions were covered still. Out of place, where they blended.

Bailey's eyes filled with tears.

One tear tracked down her cheek, and she tried to wipe it away before Raphael saw.

"What's wrong?" he asked.

"Nothing is wrong," she said, her throat tight. "Except…this is beautiful. And it's so much more than I ever thought I would have. It just feels wonderful right now, and I can't believe that something won't go horribly wrong."

It all rolled over her like a thunderstorm, lightning and rain lashing at her soul. She was in this beautiful place, this place that had only ever been a dream to her, a place she had imagined would always only be a dream, with a man who transcended fantasy. A man she hadn't known she was waiting for, a man she had never imagined she could possibly have.

She was…she was a princess. She was going to be a mother.

She was suddenly standing in a life she had never expected, one she could still barely believe she was living.

"What if I wake up and it's all just a dream?" she whispered.

He put his warm hands on her shoulders, sliding them down her bare arms, holding her tight. Then he leaned in from his position behind her, his breath hot against her neck. "Does this feel like a dream?"

"No," she said, her voice trembling now.

"Why would you think this was a dream?"

"Because. I used to have such vivid dreams when I was a child. I would go to bed hungry, and then spend all night dreaming that I was somewhere warm. About to have dinner. And then I would wake up just as hungry as I'd been when I'd gone to sleep and I would cry. Because it wasn't real. And that was when I realized it wasn't enough to dream. Because dreams aren't real, Raphael. They aren't." She swallowed hard. "When I met you…that was the first time I'd dreamed since I was a child. Only then I woke up. And you weren't any more real than all those other dreams. I was still hungry." She forced a smile. "And now I'm here, but it's just so difficult to believe that I won't wake up again and find it all gone."

He wrapped his arm around her waist, his large hand flat on her round stomach. "I am here," he said, his voice fierce. "I am your husband. I made vows to you, and I will keep them."

She nodded, unable to speak around the lump in her throat.

"This is beautiful," she said finally, dashing away another tear. "So beautiful it made me cry. So perfect... I can barely believe it." She turned to face him, his face another piece of art in a room filled with masterpieces. And she realized then that she was all his. Always and forever. That there was no self-protection to be found, and there never had been.

She loved him. With everything she was and everything she would be.

"Are you ready to go back down for dinner?"

"Yes," she said.

They began to walk back toward the stairs, and then she stopped in front of a massive clock built into a window, overlooking the city below.

The buildings were lit, casting a golden glow onto the river. She stepped up, moving nearer to it, leaning against the railing that was designed to keep people a safe distance from the glass, and gazing at the scene.

"Do you still feel like you're dreaming?" he asked, moving closer to her.

"No matter where you come from, I'm not sure this can feel real."

"A private art showing? One of the most beautiful

views in the world? That feels all too real to me. But you…you might very well be a dream."

She turned to face him, her heart thundering fast and hard. "Me? I thought it was a lot closer to a nightmare."

"Bailey," he said, and not for the first time she was struck by the absurdity of her extremely American name spoken in his cultured accent.

But he made it sound sexy. And no one else had ever managed to do that.

He pressed his hand between her shoulder blades, drawing his fingertips down the line of her spine until his hand reached the rounded curve of her butt.

Her breath hitched as his touch became more and more intimate, something about the effect of his hand over the silk making her feel extra sensitive.

He leaned in close, pressing a kiss to her neck. "I promise you—this is very real."

She closed her eyes, then forced them back open. Forced herself to keep her eyes on the incredible view below as he began to gather the fabric of her skirt into his hand. Began to draw it up her legs.

She gasped as the cool air hit her skin, and he moved his palm over the bare curve of her bottom.

Then he moved his hand, dipping it between her legs, his fingers delving beneath the edge of her panties.

"Raphael," she said, her voice a fierce whisper. "Someone might come up."

"No one is allowed to come up here." He shifted his movements, pushing his fingertips forward, grazing that sensitized bundle of nerves at the apex of her thighs. "And even if they did, I would simply order them to turn back around."

"But they'll see."

"Then let them," he said, his voice firm, authoritative. "You are my woman." There was something about that proclamation that affected her on a visceral level. He had called her his wife, he had called himself her husband. But there was something different about this. Something that laid elemental ownership that went beyond legal paperwork.

She let out a slow, shuddering breath as he continued to stroke her. "Do you...do you mean that?"

He wrapped his arm around her, grabbing hold of her chin, his forearm braced against her chest as he held her against him. "My word is law," he growled, rocking his hips forward, his hardness brushing against her.

"Of course it is. But...but I need to know."

"What do you need to know, *cara*?"

"Am I your woman? Or am I a burden? A duty?"

He hesitated for only a moment. "Everything I have was presented to me. That is my duty. What was passed to me. What I inherited. But you... I chose you."

Relief washed through her, tears prickling her eyes. She just couldn't face being a millstone around his neck. Not after her mother.

He *chose* her.

Raphael held her tight for a moment, stroking her until she was gasping for breath. Until she could hardly see straight, the city lights blurring in front of her, turning into a glittering, impressionistic work of art right before her eyes.

She clung to the railing. It was the only thing keeping her upright.

Then his fingers were replaced by his arousal, as he flexed his hips forward, pushing his erection through her slick folds.

"Bend forward," he commanded, pressing his hand against her stomach and drawing the lower half of her body back slightly as she complied with his order. He slipped his hand to her hip, holding her tight as he tested her entrance with the blunt head of him.

"We can't do this here," she said, her whisper swallowed up by the expansive room.

"Do you want to?" he asked, pressing in another inch.

She lowered her head, pleasure chasing need down her spine. "Yes." She shuddered.

"Then we can."

He pushed home then, a harsh groan on his lips as he seated himself fully inside her. He turned her face, kissing her as he established a maddeningly slow rhythm that was designed to torment her—it must have been. He kept her poised, on the brink, sending little ripples of pleasure that promised to become waves but never did, as he kept himself in firm control.

She began to rock back against him, meeting him thrust for thrust, trying to increase the pressure, to entice him to go harder, deeper, faster. And when those subtle enticements failed to fracture his command, she said the words. Over and over again, until she felt him splinter, until he began to break apart, piece by royal piece.

His hold became punishing, his blunt fingertips digging into her flesh as he pounded himself into her, over and over again. He was saying things, harsh, broken things, in a language she didn't know, his breath hot on her neck as he whispered promises her body understood even if her brain did not.

His arm was an iron bar across her chest, his grip tight at the base of her throat, while he slipped his other hand between her thighs, working wicked magic at the center of her pleasure.

"Please," he said, his voice as fractured as the rest of him. "Please. I can't hold on much longer."

His desperation, his plea, was the thing that turned the key, unleashed the flood of pleasure inside her. She came hard, a hoarse cry on her lips as her internal muscles clenched tightly around him.

He held her up as he thrust into her two more times, shaking as he cried out his own pleasure, the sound echoing off the walls around them, a new addition to the gallery that already contained so much beauty. Now it held this. Them.

Surrounded by so much history, it made everything feel more weighty. Made this feel more real. Made it feel like perhaps it wasn't just a dream.

As he held her tight, clung to her while they waited for the aftershocks to stop, she realized there was no way on earth this could be a dream. She never could have spun this out of thin air. She didn't possess the raw material to do it. Her life, that life of hunger and vague neglect, hadn't allowed her to dream of anything half so big.

And it had nothing so much to do with Paris, or the beautiful gown she was wearing, or the fact that Raphael was the most incredibly handsome man she'd ever seen. It was just him. The warm press of his chest against her back, that tight grip he kept on her. Making her so very aware of his strength, and yet so very safe at the same time.

"Would you still like to go down to dinner?" he asked, moving away from her, smoothing her dress back down and turning her to face him. He began to tuck her hair back into place, smoothing her, wiping away a smear of lipstick from below her lip.

"Is there another option?" she asked, sounding as shaky as she felt.

"Perhaps we could take that walk around the city?"

He whisked her quickly back through the museum, with such an air of command about him that no one dared to try to stop them. His hold on her was so possessive, so protective, and she gloried in it. In belonging to him. In feeling like she mattered.

"Are you going to call your driver?"

"No," he said, "we should walk."

He released his hold on her, shifting so that he could clasp her hand, just as he had done that last night in Vail, just before he had broken her heart. That simple, sweet gesture that had meant so much to her then and felt amplified now.

He led her down the sidewalk, the streets still alive even at this late hour. She had a feeling they looked out of place, she in her long black coat, her green dress shimmering around her feet, and Raphael in his tuxedo strolling along the river.

She looked up, her breath catching as she saw the Eiffel Tower in the distance, lit up for the evening.

"I never thought I would see that in person," she said.

"The Eiffel Tower?"

"It's surreal. I've seen it in so many movies…and there it is. Right in front of me."

"Then I think you will enjoy what I have in mind next."

She did. A small café just across the street from the tower. The base was visible from the little alcove they were seated in. They had coffee and simple sandwiches with bread, cheese and ham that tasted anything but simple. It wasn't the lavish, elegant dinner that they would have had if they'd stayed at the museum, but it meant more to her. It meant everything.

Hours passed that felt like minutes, and it was time to start walking back. It was late now, and her feet hurt, but she didn't want to get a car. She wanted to keep walking. She wanted to extend this night, forever. To keep existing in this moment, with the man as he was now. His guard had dropped somewhere along the way, and she wanted to keep him here.

Far too soon, they were back at the penthouse, but it was quickly clear to her that the night wasn't over. He took nearly as long getting her undressed as she had taken to get dressed before they went out.

When he pressed her into the soft mattress, he spent time thoroughly tasting each and every inch of her. Then he went over all those tender places with his hands, taking her to the brink over and over again.

When they both went over, it was together, and with all the pleasure pounding through her, images from earlier in the evening, from their time together in Colorado, mixing together inside her, painting a picture of a reality more beautiful than dreams, there was only one thing she could think to say.

"I love you."

Much later, when Bailey was asleep, Raphael stood on the balcony of the penthouse, gazing out at the city lighting up the night sky below. He wrapped his fingers tightly around the balustrade, Bailey's admission ringing inside him.

He had said nothing in return. And she had fallen asleep soon enough. But a response would be needed. Still, he could not give her the response she wanted.

If he had learned one thing about ruling from his parents, it was that there could be no greater attachment in the entire world than the attachment to the country. To the cause.

Certainly, a man could care for and treat his wife and children well, but love was an entirely separate issue. Love was something reserved for citizens, for the land and old stone buildings, the family history. Love was something much more like patriotism than what Bailey was talking about. At least, in his world.

Love kept its distance. It served others, not always those closest. His father had always made that so very clear. In the rules he established, the limited time he allowed his mother to spend with him.

When you were royalty, love wasn't personal. It was broad, spread out over everything that fell beneath your rule.

It could be expressed least of all beneath your own roof. Not in the ways that were shown on movies and in TV shows. A ruler cared for his subjects by seeing to their needs, and his father had always done much the same with Raphael and his mother.

The things he presented them with were there in his stead.

But still, he would have to say something to her.

He could say the words. They would cost him nothing.

His chest seized up tight at the thought. He had never told a single person that he loved him or her, ever. He didn't like the idea of starting now, particularly not when it was simply to soothe her feelings.

No, there had to be something else.

He took his phone out of his pocket, tapping the screen as he continued to formulate a plan in his mind. Then he dialed the palace in Santa Firenze.

"I'm going to need gifts sent up to the penthouse in Paris by tomorrow morning. A diamond necklace, flowers—enough to fill every surface in the place—and a lavish spread for breakfast. The best croissants you can find, meat, cheese. Something for the princess to drink that doesn't contain alcohol."

He cut the call off, turning and facing the doors to the penthouse. This would suffice. He would make her happy. He knew that he could. He was a man with near limitless power and deep pockets. Whatever she desired, he would give her.

He thought of her face tonight as she had looked at the art, of the way she had begun to weep with happiness. Yes, he could continue to give her things like this. Continue to make her happy. Keep her in this dream she was afraid of losing. She never had to lose it. He would make sure she didn't.

She would not be hungry with him. She would never be cold. She would never want for a damn thing.

As long as she didn't continue to ask for his love.

CHAPTER TWELVE

WHEN BAILEY WOKE up the next morning, Raphael wasn't in bed. There was something niggling at the back of her mind, but she couldn't quite think of what it was. She got up, putting on one of the silk nightgowns that were hanging in the closet. She had slept naked. Honestly, there was no point wearing clothes when Raphael was around.

Still, she was not going to walk into the living room naked.

She stopped the minute she walked out of the bedroom, shocked. There were red roses everywhere. Like grand-gesture-at-the-end-of-a-romantic-comedy level of everywhere.

She walked farther out into the room, noticing a tray set on the coffee table in front of the couch. There was a French press with coffee and a tray laden with pastries. Her stomach growled, a welcome sound after waking up too many mornings feeling vaguely nauseous.

And still, something continued to bother her.

But she figured she would work that out over some *pain au chocolat*.

"You're awake," Raphael said, striding into the room, a wide, flat velvet box clutched in his hand.

"Yes. I am. What's going on? Unless a morning order of flowers and pastries is business as usual for you. Which I kind of think might be a great tradition."

"All for you, *cara*." He moved nearer to her, holding the box up. "As is this."

Inside the box was the most incredible piece of jewelry she had ever seen. An ornate, glittering necklace composed of delicate strands of white gold braided together with gems sprinkled over it like dewdrops. And then, at the center, one large teardrop-shaped diamond that looked like it belonged at the center of a jewel heist.

And then she remembered. Last night, she had told him that she loved him. He had said nothing.

She looked around the room. This was…this was his response.

"That's…it's a lot," she said.

"Not too much for you," he said, his tone sincere, as though he were issuing her the greatest of compliments.

"Thank you," she said, waiting for…she didn't know what she was waiting for. He wasn't going to make a grand pronouncement, not today. But then, maybe it wasn't reasonable to expect one. Maybe she just needed to be patient.

"You don't sound very pleased."

He moved toward her, extending the jewelry box out to her. "I am," she said, taking it from him. "Who wouldn't want diamonds and butter?"

"Would you like to put the necklace on now?"

"No, thank you. I'm still in my pajamas. That would be a little bit ostentatious, don't you think?"

"You're free to be as ostentatious as you like," he said.

"That is a dangerous bit of permission. You have no idea what I'm going to do with it."

"I'm intrigued. I hope to see great acts of ostenta-tiousness in the near future."

"I will do what I can to oblige you."

"We are a headline this morning," he said casually. "As you suggested we might be."

"Oh," she replied, wincing a little bit. "How unflat-tering is it?"

"A couple of publications dared to be snide about how I was clearly forced to marry you. But others talked about how longingly you gazed at me during the party last night. And some of them even had photographs of us eating at the café, suggesting that the two of us clearly choose to spend time together in venues that are invisible because we enjoy each other's company, not just to court media attention."

That made her stomach sink. It made her wonder what his motivation had been for last night's impromptu walk through the city. She wondered if it had been a bit more calculated than it had appeared. She gritted her teeth, shutting that thought out. It didn't really mat-ter. What had happened in the museum, in front of the clock, the entire city down below, that had been for the two of them.

So that had to count for something.

Sure, it meant that he wanted sex.

No, it was more than that. It was.

"I'm glad that we turned out a pretty good PR per-formance," she said, keeping her tone neutral. She was still deciding how she was going to handle all of this.

What it meant that she had told him she loved him and he had responded by buying her more things.

"If you have to be in the headlines, it is best if they're favorable."

"Oh, right. I forgot that all of this was a bit beneath you."

"It's a distraction," he said.

"From what?"

"From the actual job. There should not be so much glory in running a country. It should never be about you."

"Okay, that's interesting coming from the most arrogant man I have ever met."

He lifted a shoulder. "Perhaps you see me as arrogant. But from my point of view, it seems that it would do my country no good to see their ruler as a man who did not possess the utmost confidence in everything he did. Why should they trust me if I don't trust myself?"

"Well, sometimes there is strength in asking for help."

"No, that's a lie that helpless people tell themselves. People who don't want to feel weak, when they are in a desperate position. I don't blame them. If one finds themselves in a desperate position, one must handle it as they see fit. And I suppose there is strength within that. But I am not desperate. Not now, nor have I ever been. My father ruled in this fashion. And he created a nation that was strong, one that has weathered worldwide financial crises and war, without ever entering into either. Should I seek to change the way things are?"

"I suppose not," she said, taking those words and holding them close, turning them over. It was clear to her that he felt showing weakness of any kind was detrimental. Not just to himself but to an entire nation. It was difficult to argue with that. The most she'd ever been in charge of was a goldfish.

What did she know?

"The entire country trusts in me confidently." He lowered his voice then, looking at her, something in his dark eyes softening. "You can, too."

Those words warmed her, comforted her. After a morning of feeling off balance, they were exactly what she needed to hear. Well, if an *I love you* was unavailable, anyway.

"If you say so."

"I do. And my word is law."

"Oh, Raphael." She stood up, pressing her hand to his chest, emotion coursing through her. "I do love you."

She felt him stiffen beneath her touch. But she didn't really care. And suddenly, she was well aware of how she would proceed.

He might not love her yet. But he'd *chosen* her. He'd said. So she was just going to love him. There was no other alternative. Nothing more than keeping everything stuffed down inside, and she didn't want to do that. It would hurt her far more than honesty would.

"Do you have a list of things you wish to see today?" he asked.

Her heart twisted. But she kept her smile firmly in place. "Why don't you surprise me?"

He liked that. She could see it in the satisfied expression on his face. The gesture of trust, her simple admission that he could possibly do a good job with anticipating her needs.

"That," he said, "I can do."

The week in Paris went by too quickly, and when they returned to the palace, Raphael threw himself into dealing with affairs of state. Which, she supposed, was unavoidable seeing as he ran the entire country. He had left it in the capable hands of his staff for a while, but there were most certainly things that only the prince could see to.

She told herself she wasn't lonely. That she didn't miss having him around. That it was fine that she only saw him at night when he came to bed and took her with the kind of passion he withheld from her during the other hours of the day.

Most of all, she told herself that it was okay when he didn't say he loved her, too.

Oh, he had given her absolutely everything. More clothing than she could conceivably wear, especially considering it was maternity wear, and she would only need it for a few more months. Jewelry, books and then last week, an entire wing of the palace. All for her.

One day he had come in with a petite woman clutching a book at his side. "I know that back in Colorado we had discussed you finishing your degree," he said. "I have employed a teacher to assist you. She has compiled accredited curriculum and a university you can work with remotely. I want to make sure you have everything that you were promised and more."

The woman had smiled, looking down at Bailey's increasingly obvious bump. "Of course, we will work around your schedule," she said kindly. "I would not want you to feel overtaxed, Princess."

Nobody had ever cared if she was overtaxed when she was going to the University of Colorado. Nobody had cared that she was sick and tired of waiting tables when she had gotten pregnant before she had a title. Nobody at all.

It was strange to have people care so much about her condition.

And care they did. From the media to the staff at the palace, everyone was doting on her.

She had become a kind of icon for style when it came to pregnancy, but she really didn't feel like she could claim the glory for that. Raphael had appointed her a stylist who assisted her every time she went on an outing. If it were up to her, she would probably be in sweats. Though she had to concede that it wasn't really any more work to put on a dress and leggings.

She was very well taken care of. Possibly more than she had ever been in her entire life. But she still felt… empty. Because things weren't love. All of this wasn't love. It was deference, and it was…well, it was definitely care. But it wasn't what she felt for Raphael.

If there was no baby, she would have wanted him. If there was no title, and there was no expectation about marriage, she still would have wanted him. She had wanted him when she had thought he was just some kind of middle managing pharmaceutical rep.

But he hadn't wanted her. And even though he was doing a wonderful job of taking care of her now, even though he clearly still wanted her, she had doubts. And those doubts were insidious.

The doctor visit today had yielded results she knew would make him happy. The fact that she was having a boy. The kind of heir men like him were best off with. Or so she'd heard.

For some reason she was having a hard time finding the right moment to tell him.

"How are your studies going?" he asked, coming into the room that night.

"They're going very well. Professor Johnson has been extremely patient and helpful. I feel like I haven't even really fallen behind, because getting the one-on-one help has been so valuable."

"Perfect. What exactly are you going to do with a business degree?"

"Well, back when I was in Colorado I imagined that I might open my own business someday. And I thought it might just help me get more comfortable jobs until then. Maybe with slightly better pay."

"And now?"

"I feel like it's still valuable to understand the way things work. To understand a bit about the structure of these things, and where it all fits in with the economy. Surely there's value in that for a princess."

"If you find it valuable, then it is. And I'm sure that you can use it in any way you see fit. There are plenty of different charities you can get involved with. Organizations that would benefit from your insight, I'm sure. But I think a degree is one of the least things you have to offer something like that."

She sensed she was on the cusp of receiving a compliment, and so she pressed further. "Is that right?"

"You are fiercely determined. And a wonderful advocate. I can imagine you will get a great deal done. An iron will combined with the title is a wonderful thing."

"I'm glad you can appreciate my iron will."

"I appreciate it much more now that it isn't being turned on me with as much frequency."

She laughed. "Well, I make no guarantees."

Silence stretched between them, strange and slightly uncomfortable. She was so rarely uncomfortable with him anymore. She imagined it was because this silence was full of so many unsaid things. She wanted to tell him that she loved him again. Just to see what he would say. She told him every day. Had since that day in Paris. There had been no response. No response beyond giving her more and more.

"I have a very busy schedule tomorrow," he said, for no reason that she could discern.

"So, I won't see you?"

"Probably not."

"I haven't seen you enough lately," she said.

"I am very busy," he said, his tone getting hard. "It is something you will have to get accustomed to. I was around a little more than I would normally be when I first brought you back here out of courtesy to you. And because we were planning a wedding. And then, of course, we went to Paris, so we saw a great deal of each other. But it cannot continue. You will find a great many things to keep yourself busy."

"Is that why you're keeping me in school? Is that why you're talking to me about what I might do with my degree and all my spare time?"

"Yes, in part. You need to have something to keep you occupied. Something that will enable you to serve the country."

"I will also be parenting our child."

"Yes," he said, speaking slowly. "But mostly that responsibility will fall to nannies."

"No," she said, "it most certainly will not."

"You have a duty to the country, Bailey."

"I have a duty to our baby. Above and before anything else. I was ready to be a single mother, Raphael, because I had no idea if I would ever see you again. In my mind, I reshaped my entire life to accommodate this child. And while it seemed daunting, while I still don't know if I'm even half qualified to be a mother, I know that I want to devote my time to that."

"But it is not how it's done. Both because we will be busy ruling the nation, and because our child must be set on the right path from the first day, as I was."

"Being…bowed to by servants and held only by members of staff? Both worshipped and ignored all at the same time?"

"I was never ignored," he said, his tone hard. "I was essential. The heir to the throne. It will be the same for our child, and every portion of their childhood will be spent building to the moment they shall stand as I do, the prince or princess of Santa Firenze. It is how it has always been, and how it must continue to be."

"I don't care how it's been done for the past hundred years. I'm also the first nobody anyone in your storied royal lineage has married. Expect that I will do things differently. That I will have different expectations."

"So, your childhood was idyllic?"

"No," she said, "my childhood was awful. And you know that. My mother was eternally stressed and filled with resentment for me. She worked a job she hated and barely managed to keep us fed and clothed. We had no relationship. We have no relationship now. She resents me far too much for that. She made the decision to have me, and she regretted it ever since."

"So why," he said, his tone full of exasperation, "do you think the key to our child's happiness is you being around?"

"I don't think you understand. When I found out I was pregnant, I knew that I was in the exact same situation my mother was in. I knew that it would be so easy

for me to spend my child's entire life resenting them.
For interrupting my plans. For making things difficult.
But they were my choices that led to that, Raphael, and
I refused to punish my child for them. I thought long
and hard about how I was going to avoid repeating the
pattern that I had seen myself falling into. It was so important to me. But I realized, a few days after I found
out I was pregnant, as I was lying in bed crying, ready
to rend my garments in my distress, that it wouldn't be
that way as long as I loved my child. As long as I loved
my child more than I loved the dreams that I had built
for myself. As long as I love my child more than my
own comfort."

"Your child will be comfortable."

"But I want to be with them. I'm not going to fill up
my days with busywork when I could be spending time
with him or her. I like the idea of volunteering. I like
the idea of having something of a vocation other than
princess. But I'm not turning over the entire responsibility of my child to someone else."

"But it is how things are done." She could tell he was
reaching the end of his temper. That he didn't understand—even after all this time with her—dealing with
someone who wouldn't simply accept his word as law.

"Don't *you* want to spend time with our child?"

He waved a hand. "It has nothing to do with want,
and everything to do with responsibility. It was thus
for my parents, and it will be thus for me. You talk of
love as if it is some kind of magic. As if it will move
mountains, create time and keep a kingdom standing,
but it is not. It is a potential distraction. Something that
might prevent a ruler from acting in the best interest

of his country. I cannot allow that. My father did not, and so I must not."

Her heart was pounding faster now, her stomach turning over. "You really think that love is the enemy?"

"I think it is an unnecessary distraction. I think a man in my position can afford to love nothing more than his country."

Those words hit hard, and she was reminded of that moment in the hotel room the night he'd first ended things with her. That grim finality. The evidence that he would not be moved. Not by tears or flying shoes.

"So, you'll never love me." It wasn't a question but a statement. Even as she spoke the words, they felt sharp in her throat, cutting into her, making it hard to breathe. "You're only ever going to love this country. You're not even going to love your own child?"

She had been willing to live in a situation where he didn't love her. Had been willing to try to figure that out. But the realization that he expected to have nothing to do with his own son or daughter was something she couldn't easily sweep under the rug.

"I told you this child mattered to me. There is a reason I had to marry you and not simply find someone else—"

"Will you love him?"

"I have never said those words to anyone," he said. "It has never been important to my existence."

"It is important now, Raphael. It's important to me."

"Have I not demonstrated how deeply I care for you?" he roared. "Have I not given everything to you that you could possibly want? And still, you behave as though it isn't enough."

"Raphael—"

"No. You are a waitress," he said, his tone harsh. "And I brought you here, to my palace, into my home, and I gave you all that it was in my possession to give. Still, you act as though somehow I am beneath you. You accuse me of being arrogant, and yet I think you best me on that score. Have I not given you an entire wing of this palace that has been in my family for generations? Did I not make you a DeSantis princess? You lived in a hovel, and I have elevated you in ways you never could have aspired to, and this is how you respond?"

"You're angry because I fail to be honored by the scraps that you've given me?" Rage was vibrating through her now, and she wasn't thinking entirely clearly. She didn't really care. She wanted to strike out at him. Wanted to hurt him the way that he had hurt her, all those countless times from that moment when he'd left her lying in the snow in Colorado. "That's what they are, and you have no idea. You think you can appease me with gold dust. Shiny things I never even wanted. That I should be grateful. But these are easy things, Raphael. So easy. For a man in your position, giving me a wing of your palace is nothing. You couldn't walk the length of it in an afternoon, so how will you ever miss a quadrant of rooms? You send me gifts, gifts that you have ensured I know are not extravagant enough to put a dent in your royal treasury. And you act as though you are somehow doing me a great favor. But how many necklaces can a woman wear? How many beautiful gowns?"

"That isn't the point," he said, sounding frustrated.

"Yes," she said, "it is the point. These things…they are easily replaceable. They are easily acquired for a man like you. But love? That is…it is so rare. And it is so beautiful. And so very, very costly. Don't you think that it has cost me every time I have told you that I love you and you've said nothing in return? That is a gift beyond price, and you don't even see it. You don't see everything that *I* have given to you. My body, my soul, my heart. I left my dreams, modest though they were, my dreams that you felt were somehow nothing, to come here and be with you."

Her angry words did nothing to cool his rage. "Look at all you have been given in return. Don't ask me to feel sorry for you. Don't pretend that you didn't love what we had in Paris. You didn't enjoy the extravagance."

"Of course I did. I'm only human. But all it will take is a financial crisis, a natural disaster, a war to wipe these things out. They are temporary. They are nothing. If the world catches fire, they'll burn away. And then what will be left? All that will be left standing is you and me, and without all of these shows of wealth and magnificence you don't know how to connect with me. You don't know who you are."

"But that will not happen," he said, his voice hard.

"Hopefully not. But you're still missing the point. These things are temporary. And they're not real. Not really. What I've given for you, that's real. What I feel for you? It *hurts*. It hurts whenever I breathe. It strips me of my pride by inches, day after day, every time I tell you I love you and you say nothing back. And what cost have I been to you? Truly."

"You are obsessed with that," he spat. "The cost. You wish to be an inconvenience? You wish to seem so high maintenance?"

"No. I wish to know that I'm not the only one sacrificing to have this. I wish to be something more than one of your possessions that you take out and put away at your will. That is what I want."

He exploded then. "You wish for the impossible. You wish to control how I feel. You have decided that my actions are not good enough. What good would it be if I felt things, and yet did nothing for you? If I told you that I loved you, and yet left you in that heap of an apartment in Colorado. Then you would not find these gestures so empty. If there was a lack of them, I imagine you would be saying that I clearly didn't love you because of what I failed to do."

"It's true," she said, her voice small. "I feel like those things kind of have to come together for them to matter."

"Is this how you were as a child?" he asked, the question hitting her like a slap. "Never able to be pleased? If your mother took care of you, but failed to demonstrate to you that her love was real, did you resent her?" His words dug beneath her skin, hit at her insecurity. But that wasn't fair. She refused to feel guilty for wanting someone to love her.

"That was low," she said, her voice vibrating. "Even for you, that was so damn low."

"It isn't throwing a shoe, I grant. But it's something to consider." He turned, his broad back filling her vision as he began to walk away.

"You're leaving now?" she asked.

"I can't talk to you at the moment. And so I refuse to."

"And your word is law," she said.

He turned again. "Yes," he said. "Yes, it is. And you would do well to remember that."

"Or what? You'll send me back to where I came

from? What does it matter if we are still together if you aren't even going to have me raise our child? If I don't mean anything to you?"

"I want you with me," he said.

"But why? To hear you tell it, I am nothing more than a waitress, and I am beneath you. You don't love me, and you never will. You don't need me to be there for our child. You think everything I came from is insignificant, that everything I want is something that doesn't matter. Why do you want me with you?"

He crossed the space between them, his expression lean and feral. "Because I want *you*," he growled, wrapping his arm around her and pulling her up against his body. It was hard and hot, everything she loved about him. Everything that always saw her weakening in his presence. She had to resist him now. She had to.

"It isn't enough. It's just another thing that will burn away."

"Never," he said, pressing his lips to her neck.

"Yes," she said, "it will. My body will change after I have this baby, and the years will soften it even more. I won't look like I did when you met me, when you first decided you wanted me. I'll be like every other old, unneeded thing littering this palace. And I will not submit myself to that."

"Have I not told you that your strength is valuable to me?"

"You have. But it isn't enough."

"And nothing less than what you want is enough?" He released his hold on her, taking a step back.

"Exactly. I've given you all that I am. All that I ever will be. I have submitted my future to you. And in return I want to know you. I want to have you. Every part of you. I want your love, I want your anger, I want everything messy and imperfect inside of you. I don't just want this distant arrogance, this blind insistence that you are law and above everything. I don't want it. I want all of that broken down and destroyed."

"Then you will never have it," he said.

She moved to him then, gripping his face, closing the distance between them and kissing him with all the pent-up rage that was inside her. Every twisted, ugly thing. All her selfishness, all her need. Her insecurity and her fear. And always, even now, every last bit of her love.

"Don't hide from me," she said, her voice vibrating.

"There is nothing to hide," he responded, his dark eyes blank.

"Liar," she said, claiming his mouth again.

He had told her more than once that she made him burn. That she had control over him no one else ever had.

Well, if ever he needed to go up in flames, it was now. And she was going to make sure it happened.

CHAPTER THIRTEEN

RAPHAEL KNEW THAT he should push her away. That he could not allow her to try to gain control in this way. He was Prince Raphael DeSantis, and no woman could manipulate him.

Except he could not bring himself to pull her lush mouth away from his. Could not deny the fire that burned between them.

He was being ripped apart from the inside out, piece by piece, and still, he could not bring himself to push her away. Still, he could not deny the desire that burned between Bailey and himself.

He would show her. He would prove to her, with this, that the need between them was enough. That it transcended use, that it went somewhere beyond beauty. There had been many beautiful women in his life. He'd always had his pick.

When he'd seen her, something had streaked through him, white hot and clean. It had been different than anything else ever had been. More. Deeper. It had been real. Real in a way nothing else before it had ever been. He would make her see. He would make her understand.

Raphael grabbed hold of her hair, twisting his fingers through the silken strands, tugging hard as he continued to kiss her, deep and long. As he took her seduction and flipped it against her.

Love.

They didn't need love. He didn't need it. It didn't matter. It wasn't important. And for a man in his position, it wasn't even possible. He had never wanted for it. Never once. He had always been given everything he needed.

But never love. Therefore, he could only assume that love was not among the necessary. Not for a man like him. If it were, his parents would have given him that, but they hadn't. Instead, he had been given education. He had been given staff. He had been given a room filled with the kinds of toys that would ignite any child's delight.

As a teenager, he had been given new cars. Well-fitted suits and private tutors who instructed him on how to best conduct himself in all situations.

Unlike Bailey, he had never been cold. He had never gone without. He'd had everything, always.

How dare this little witch come in and tell him that he lacked? How dare she make it seem as though he lived with a deficit? How dare she reduce everything that had always mattered to him to insignificant rubble? How dare she brush aside his gestures so casually?

He would not allow it. Not again. Not ever again. His blood was liquid fire in his veins as he ran his hands over her curves, reveling in her softness, in her heat. In her obvious need for him.

Yes, that was what he needed. He needed to feel how much she wanted him. And he needed it now.

He pushed his hands up beneath her skirt, his fingertips sliding easily beneath the edge of her panties. He felt that she was wet for him. Even angry, she still wanted him.

"You want me ugly?" he asked, his voice rough. "You want me out of control?"

He would give her all that and more. Here. Now. With his body. He would make her pay for this. For making him feel like his insides were made entirely of broken glass. For taking his well-ordered life and turning it completely upside down. For taking his perfect existence and proving to him that it was something less.

Yes. He would make her pay for that.

He pushed a finger deep inside her, watched as her mouth fell open, her eyes glazing over with pleasure. Yes, he wanted her like this. Mindless for him as he was for her, every damn day. Every moment, every breath. He wanted her to feel this desperation. To feel like it was all slipping away and there was nothing she could do about it. To feel hungry, aching, empty. As though nothing could ever fill the void. That was his entire existence with her. He wanted her to know that. To understand.

He had never felt like this. Everything he'd wanted, he'd had. And she insisted on keeping herself just out of reach. On making his best efforts not good enough.

She was ruining them. She was ruining him.

He would return the favor.

"Is this what you want," he rasped, adding a second finger to the first, rubbing the sensitive bundle of nerves at the apex of her thighs with his thumb. "You want me out of control?"

"I've *had* you out of control," she said. "From the beginning. But you won't admit what that means."

"It's sex. That's what it means. That we have very, very good sex."

He withdrew his fingers from her, rubbing her hips, sliding his hands down her thighs and lifting her, wrapping her legs around his waist, carrying her to the bed. He kissed her then, deep and long, with every ounce of his passion, every bit of his rage.

"No," she said, and he paused in his movements. "No, it's not sex. You chose me. You chose me, and that matters."

He said nothing, ignoring the pain those words inflicted on his heart as he pushed her skirt up her hips, dragging her panties down. Then he freed himself from his slacks. He didn't bother with more foreplay. Didn't bother with gentility. Instead, he thrust deep inside her, both of them gasping as he went deep. She was so tight, so wet and so undeniably his.

She could love him all she wanted. She did love him. Why couldn't that be enough for her? He didn't understand.

Don't you?

The howling beast inside him supplied the question, and he rejected it. Rejected all thought in favor of feeling. The feeling of her, the heat of her body, tight around him, the feeling of her fingernails digging into his skin. The sound of her needy cries as he pushed them both harder, higher. The feel of her hot breath against his neck as she panted, signs that she was getting closer to her peak.

That was his truth. It was all he cared about. He would exist in it now. Live in this moment, for as long as he could. He wanted nothing else. Nothing else, ever.

She was wrong. Wrong about him. Because if everything else was stripped away. If he ended up a prince with no palace, no kingdom, they would still have this.

She will love you. She will pour everything out for you. And what will you give in return?

He gritted his teeth, thrusting harder, losing himself in the fractured rhythm that only the two of them could ever dance to. The flames rose higher inside him, and he didn't fight it. He let it consume him, his release a shock of thunder inside him, shaking him, rattling him to his core. And as he spilled himself inside her, she found her own bliss. Her internal muscles clenched tightly around him, wringing more pleasure out of him, prolonging his orgasm.

It was always so with her. All of these things that he had never thought possible. That he had never thought to want.

And the truth of it all hung somewhere between them, hovered over him like a cloud, and he was desperate to hide from it. To push it away. Because those three words were the undoing of his entire life. Those three words undermined everything he was, everything he believed. They would shatter him. Utterly, completely.

He could not allow it.

He pushed himself away from her, forking his fingers through his hair, pacing the length of the room.

"I love you," she said.

He turned, that thing inside him savaging him now, tearing him to shreds from the inside out. "No!" He roared the words at her, satisfied when her face contorted with fear. With anguish. Because he had to make her see. He had to make her see that this would not happen. That it could not.

"But I do." The simplicity of it…that was the worst

part. As though it simply had been and now always would be. As though he had no control at all.

"You shouldn't," he said. "No one ever has. Why should you? Why should you find it so easy to love me?"

"An entire nation loves you."

"Because of what I was born to be. Not because of who I am." Those words were far too heavy. They landed against the top of the well he kept covered. That bottomless, needy well that contained the dark truth about himself. About who he was and what that meant.

He never wanted it to open. He never wanted that truth to come out.

"I love you," she said again, defying his orders at every turn, as she always did.

Bailey, so strong and defiant, always. How had she become his? How had she decided that she loved him? How had she decided that she could love at all? With a life as bleak and difficult as hers sounded, how had she arrived at the conclusion that love meant anything?

He could ask her. But his mouth wouldn't form the words.

There was no point to them anyway. There was no point to any of this. It had all been a fiction from the very beginning. A dream.

Bailey talked a lot about dreams. About how she'd been afraid to have them. He had spent his life living an existence carefully constructed to appear like a dream, the kind of life that prevented him from having any aspiration that fell outside duty.

He had no idea what it was to dream. To want. To hope for anything that extended beyond what was expected. He had no idea at all.

She was his first dream. She had been from the moment he had walked into that diner. His first foray into something that went beyond necessity and into desire.

He closed that off, ruthlessly, with great finality. He could not allow himself to think such things. It was nonnegotiable.

She was exactly what his father had always told him something like this would be. A distraction. She was a fatal weakness, something that could get right under his skin, changing everything he was, everything he was supposed to believe in.

She would become larger than Santa Firenze in his heart, in his mind, and he could not allow it.

"I don't love you," he said, his voice rough. "I never will."

Then he turned and walked out of the room, leaving behind a piece of himself he had never known existed. Leaving behind the most essential, vital part of his heart. But it was for the best. It was all he could do.

The only other option would make his world fall apart. And he couldn't allow that. Not when so much depended on him standing firm.

He felt in that moment that if there were a snowbank for him to throw himself into, he would do it.

The door to Bailey's room opened behind him, and he turned. She was there, her blue eyes glittering.

"I don't know what you think my response will be," she said. "If I will accept it and tell you that's okay. If I will continue on in this farce of a relationship simply because you will it, and your word is law. But I don't care about your pride, Raphael. Your pride needs to burn. If it's the thing that separates us, then it is the thing that has to go. I'm not staying."

"You have to."

"I will call the American embassy and tell them you're holding me captive."

"After we appeared in Paris together? After our wedding? The entire world knows you're carrying my child, Bailey. Do you honestly think you can pull something like that off?"

"I will, because I have to. Because you have finally killed the hope that I've been holding on to for all of these months. You built my trust back up, and now you've destroyed it again. And I'm not going to give you another chance. If you want to be involved in our child's life, you can. But you're going to have to come and visit us in Colorado. Because that's where I live. That's my world. And even if you never understand why it matters to me, that's the life I built for myself. It is not small. And neither am I."

She sucked in a sharp breath before continuing. "I was never just a waitress. I was never just anything. I have always, always been Bailey Harper. And that has always mattered. I pulled myself up with all of my own strength, and I will be damned if you reduce all of that effort to nothing. It will be good enough for my child, because it is what I built. And there will be love in my house. If your duty, or whatever you feel, is compelling enough to bring you across the world to visit, then I'll be happy with that. But I sincerely doubt anything less than love would compel a person to make that kind of effort. So I'll expect that you simply won't be involved."

"You can't do that," he said. "My child is my heir. The heir to this throne. He must be raised here. He must know of his heritage."

"A heritage of ice. A heritage so cold it will destroy him as soon as he touches it? No. That isn't the life that

I want for our child. And someday I think you'll see that I'm right. When your son grows up to be a more compassionate, more loving, more caring ruler than you will ever be. When he becomes the husband that you have been afraid to be."

"My son?"

"Yes. I had a doctor appointment today. And I was going to tell you. But then we fought."

"You tell me that you're having my son and are going to take him away from me?"

"You're taking him away from yourself, Raphael. That's the truth of it. But you don't want him. Not really."

"I do." He did. With everything. He didn't understand what was happening to him. Why he felt so torn, so bloody. So close to being destroyed.

"You like the idea of a wife. You like the idea of a son that you can raise and mold in your image. But you will always keep us at a distance. And I won't let that happen. You can break down that wall inside of you, that thing that keeps you from lowering yourself to accept my love."

"It has nothing to do with lowering myself."

"Maybe not. But you still won't do it. You're too proud."

"What are your demands?"

"Ready a jet to fly me back home. Arrange for me to gain entry into the US, and I will not make a scandal out of this. But I swear to you, I will strike your pride in any way that I can if you don't comply. Because I know that's the only thing you truly value."

Raphael could only stand there, stunned, wounded. And then he knew there was only one answer he could give her. That there was only one right thing to do. And it had nothing to do with pride and everything to do with the fact that he finally saw what she had been telling him from the beginning. What he had done to her was an insult. He had taken her, manipulated her and had never bothered to look deeper into his actions because he knew that doing so would require him to face deep, uncomfortable truths about his life and about himself that he had never wanted to face.

And so he did the only thing he could do. The only thing he could do and still survive.

"I will ready the jet. Be ready to leave early tomorrow."

Then he turned and walked away. Because he would be damned if he watched her leave.

CHAPTER FOURTEEN

HE WONDERED HOW a palace with so many people in it could feel empty. But it did. With Bailey gone it was empty.

And so was he.

He wandered the halls of the place he'd been so absurdly proud to bring her to. As if she would see it and crumble in humility and gratefulness because it was a palace, and there was no way she could have ever aspired to such a thing on her own.

She had worked for her life. For her education. For that apartment he'd insulted. He'd worked for none of this and yet held it up as some form of achievement.

Dio.

He was every bit as arrogant and unrelenting as she'd accused him of being.

But it was the only thing he had. The only thing that stood between him and the yawning void he tried so desperately to keep covered up.

It had cracked open now, and he was so terribly conscious of just how vacant and empty his entire existence was.

It made him question what he'd been taught. For the first time, he questioned his father. He'd never wanted to.

He'd so desperately wanted to preserve that image. Of a man who ruled a country with unfailing strength, who was the leader that Raphael had always aspired to be.

But he had been a terrible father and an even worse husband.

Raphael gritted his teeth, lowering his head and bracing himself against the wall. His staff continued to walk by, not speaking, not pausing. Why should they? That was the environment he'd continued to foster.

No connections. Nothing to interrupt business as usual.

Deference as a replacement for connection.

Prizing efficiency in a grand spectrum of days that all blurred together, instead of lingering in human connection.

He was breaking apart inside, and there was no one here to talk to. No one who would ever pause to ask why.

Oh, his Secret Service would take a bullet for him. But they would never talk to him.

Because that was what his father had taught him. What had been ingrained in him from childhood. He had never questioned it.

Never questioned when his father had yelled at his mother late one night for skipping an event because Raphael had been sick.

He knew he hadn't meant for Raphael to hear the argument, but he had.

"I needed you there tonight, and you were not. It split my focus!"

"Your son was sick," she hissed. *"I needed to be with him."*

"We have staff for that. An excellent staff. The boy wants for nothing. I, however, looked weak in front of

*the ambassadors. Everyone's wife was in attendance
except for you. You knew what this marriage was to be.
You are to support Santa Firenze first. Above all else.
Anything else is a distraction."*

The next day he'd had a new toy. A gift from his father. The only contact the older man made during his
illness. And after that his mother had been even more
distant than before. An edict given by his father, because his son and heir could not be made dependent.

He'd done his best not to be a distraction. There and
then he'd purposed to be the sort of man his father was.
He never wanted his mother to be on the receiving end of
his father's wrath for something concerning him, either.

The fault was his. It couldn't possibly be the old
prince's. Not when the man was such a brilliant leader,
not when he had done so much for the country.

He was also forced to remember the day his mother
died. When his father had stood, stoic beside the grave
of his late wife, and Raphael, only fifteen, had kept his
face as hard as the old man's.

"Grief is a distraction, Raphael," he said later. *"A
weakness only other men can afford. You must never
love anything more than you love your country."*

"You don't?" he asked.

*"No. And a good thing, because the nation won't
pause for the loss of your mother. And neither can I."*

Neither can you.

That had been the unspoken subtext of the conversation. That loss could never touch men like them. Because living life dictated by emotions was to walk on
unsteady ground. He'd understood it.

And yet now he felt that even if it made sense, even
if his father was right in his way, he was also wrong.

This kind of cold emptiness would break a man in the end. At least, it would break him. He was broken now, that was certain. Without Bailey, who had been the world's biggest distraction from the first moment he'd met her. The first spark of the unexpected in a lifetime of grim certainty.

Duty without love was empty. Life without love was empty. He could see that clearly now.

There was no cost to it. Bailey was right. If it cost nothing, it meant nothing. If you hid behind walls of control, and kept your wife and children at a distance, appeasing them with gifts…there was no love at all.

It didn't protect your country. It only protected you.

Building a wall like that, keeping out the elements… it could protect. But a life without sunlight could only leave you cold.

He had allowed it to make him a statue long before he'd been memorialized in death.

His father hadn't loved the country most. He'd loved himself and his protection most, and he'd taught Raphael to do the same.

He thought back to his mother's funeral. How much he would have given to get a hug from his father then. But the old man couldn't bend that way. Not for Santa Firenze, for his pride.

It had seemed like strength to Raphael then. But he could see now that the greatest strength would have been in showing weakness. For a son grieving his mother. A nation mourning a princess.

Instead, Raphael had been given a new car the next day.

A single moment sharing their loss would have been

so much more costly to his father. So much more valuable to Raphael.

The gifts had always been empty, but Raphael had wanted them to matter. So he'd believed his father. Believed him so that he could pretend he'd been loved.

You have been loved. You've been loved from the start by Bailey Harper, and just like your father, you pushed it away.

He pressed his hand to his chest, trying to staunch the flow of pain bleeding endlessly from his heart.

He had pushed away the best gift he'd ever received, because the cost of it had been too great.

What good was endless wealth if he couldn't afford love?

That was the damned rub. He couldn't buy love. He had to pay for it with the same. With humility and sacrifice. With discomfort. With his very soul.

As he looked around the palace and saw nothing but empty vanity, he knew that he had no other choice.

Her dream was over.

That was her predominant thought as the plane touched down in Colorado. It was what played in her mind over and over again as the car that Raphael had organized for her picked her up from the airport and drove her to a neighborhood that was unfamiliar.

"This isn't my house," she said when the driver pulled her up to a place with a well-manicured lawn that she had never seen in her life.

"These are the keys," he said. "My instructions were to bring you here and to give you these. Raphael said there would be an explanation inside."

Heart hammering, she took the keys from the driver's

hand and made her way up the front walk. She put the key in the lock, and it turned. She took a deep breath before walking inside. And then she did. It was beautiful. Modest, and certainly not a palace. But exactly the kind of place she had dreamed she might find herself in one day.

There was an envelope on the counter with her name written on it. She opened it, pulling out a simple note that was inside.

I know that you won't want to take this from me. I know that it will offend your pride. However, please consider this part of my child support. I am a prince after all, so you know that I can well afford it. This is the dream that you spoke about more than once when we were together. A house in a nice neighborhood. I wanted to make sure that you had this. That our child had this.

It wasn't signed. It didn't need to be. It could only be from one person. He was arrogant even when giving houses as parting gifts.

Her heart crumpled, and she looked around the room, feeling so adrift. This had been her dream. This little house, this kind of security. But it didn't feel like enough now. And that had nothing to do with the fact that she had just spent the last month being a princess. The last month living in a palace. No, all the feelings of inadequacy had to do with the fact that she had spent the last month sharing a bed with Raphael. And there was no room for him in this little house. In this little life.

Not for the first time, she wondered if she simply should have accepted what he'd given. Wondered if it would have been enough. If she shouldn't have pressed for more.

She shook that thought off quickly.

There was nothing else she could do, not really. It had been the right thing. The right thing for herself, and for her baby.

Anyway, it was too late to question it now. But this gesture, this one last gesture, which wasn't a whole giant mansion or anything crazy like Raphael would normally do, was the first sign she'd really seen that he had actually listened to her at all. That he saw value in her dream. Beauty in it the same way that she had.

It was a little bit late now, but she would accept it. Maybe, just maybe, he was starting to understand a little bit. Maybe there was still hope.

Or that's just what you want to think because you spent the entire plane ride back here crying and feeling like you'd been stabbed through the heart.

Yes, there was that. That couldn't be ignored.

She did feel a little bit stabbed.

The days began to bleed together. She went to class and came back home. She wasn't working, because she was allowing Raphael to pay for a few things. Maybe that was wrong. But he was the father of her baby and currently still her husband. They weren't going to divorce officially until after the baby was born. All contact she'd had with him had been made through his aides. She saw no reason to go against him on that. Mostly, she just didn't have the energy. She was close to six months pregnant, undeniably so, and unable to muster up much energy to do anything. Though she had a feeling the heartbreak was to blame, more than the pregnancy.

She sighed heavily, throwing her purse down onto the couch, her body following quickly after. This place was starting to feel like home. Maybe that was a betrayal, seeing as it had come from Raphael. But it was one of the few bright spots in her life. This gift from him that was still extravagant by the standards of most people, but actually showed his willingness to listen.

She heard footsteps and sat up, her heart hammering hard. She was pretty sure she was hallucinating. Except then she looked toward her bedroom and saw a glorious figure standing there. He was wearing the same sort of well-cut suit that he always wore, his expression as lovely and arrogant as ever.

She felt like she was having déjà vu. Flashing back to the moment he had been in her apartment that first time he'd come to find her after their breakup. She felt like maybe she was dreaming, just as she had imagined she might be back then. She pinched herself.

"What are you doing?"

"Making sure that I'm not asleep."

"You are not," he said, taking a step toward her. It was then that she saw he did look different than he usually did. She noticed that he had dark circles under his eyes, and that the lines by his mouth were more pronounced than they usually were. It was then she noticed how exhausted he was. That his hair was disheveled as though he had been constantly running his fingers through it. It was then she realized just how affected he was by all of this. The same as she was.

"What are you doing here? I didn't realize that part of the deal with you buying me a house meant that you got to come and go in and out of it as you please."

"That was never my intent," he said, his voice rough.

"It was my intent to leave you alone. To honor what you said to me. It was my intent to let you go. But I have spent the past couple of weeks in agony, and I... I needed to see you."

"So we can have the same fight? So we can yell at each other some more? You can say more hurtful things, and I can counter with meaner things."

"No," he said, sounding ragged. "That isn't what I want. It's as far removed from what I want as anything ever could be."

"Why are you here?"

Suddenly, Raphael dropped down, landing on his knees, looking up at her with dark, tortured eyes. "I came to bow."

"You came to...what?" Her heart hammered wildly, her hands shaking. She couldn't reconcile what she was seeing in front of her. This proud, arrogant man, on his knees before her. As though he were the servant, and she were royalty.

"I was bowed to from birth," he said. "Not because anyone cared especially much, not because they were awed by their....deep emotion for me. But because of my blood. I was given everything from the moment I entered this world simply because I am a DeSantis. I have never, not once, debased myself for another human being. I will crawl across broken glass if it means having you, Bailey. I would spend the rest of my life on my knees before you if that was what it took."

She put her hands on her temples, hardly able to believe what was happening. "Raphael...you never had to do this. This was never what I wanted."

"But it is what must happen. I have been the most unbending, inflexible person, and I realize that. But I have been afraid that if I were to ever bend, I would break completely. And when you left, I did. I shattered. And I have spent the last two weeks trying to figure out what to do with the pieces of myself that you left behind. I have spent the last weeks trying to figure out what all of this means. Why your declarations of love offended me so much. Why I couldn't give them back. Why I had never…why I had never heard them before. Why I had never spoken them."

"Oh, Raphael." It hit her then, just then, that he had never felt chosen, either. That he had been born, and his fate had been set. But no one had ever chosen him.

She was from nothing and nowhere, and he was from a family as old as time, and they shared the same pain. Hers covered with pride and determination, his with arrogance and the insulation provided by his position.

But it was all pain.

"My father told me," he said, his voice breaking, "he told me that a ruler must never love anything more than he loved his country. Day after day he told me this. He told me this every time he had not a moment to spare to say a few words to me. He told me this every time he and my mother were traveling for my birthday. Every time I had dinner by myself. Except for the household staff. And in the place of my parents' presence would always be gifts. Everything a young boy could ever want."

"Gifts meant a lot to you," she said, her voice muted. Suddenly she felt…she felt foolish for not seeing that. For not realizing that for him those things had meant something. "Raphael, I am so sorry I didn't know."

"Of course not. But you see—they had to mean something to me. They were all I had. That and the… edict to always stand strong. My father told me that I couldn't allow love or grief to distract me. Even at my mother's funeral."

She put her hand over her mouth and shook her head. "No. I…how old were you?"

"Fifteen."

"He didn't comfort you or…or anything?"

"He bought me a car."

"To replace your mother?"

He shook his head slowly. "I think he bought me a car because it was…all he could really give. That was what I learned to place importance in. That and the title. The directive that was placed before me. And after he died… I told myself the only thing that mattered was ruling over my country in a way that would make my father proud. Making myself invulnerable so that I could be the best leader that I could be. To me, that's what it meant. And you have to understand that everything you said undermined that. If gifts are truly empty gestures, if things do not compensate for human connection, if arrogance and confidence are not the same as emotion, then I am a hollow, empty person with no connection at all. My father never said that he loved me. But I was able to take those things and create words from them. To fashion sentiments out of them that didn't exist. And you challenged that. From the moment that you first walked into my life."

She swallowed hard. "I'm sure that your father loved you." She wasn't sure. Because she wasn't sure her own mother had loved her. She could hardly speak for his father.

Raphael shook his head, pushing himself to his feet. "I don't think he did. But it doesn't matter to me, not now. That was part of my rock-bottom experience, you understand. I had to lay there on the floor for a while and fully come to terms with that. To accept what you had done to my worldview. To me. I got so angry at you because if what you said was true, then it meant my entire life was so much hollower than I had ever realized. If what you said was true, then I was never truly loved."

"You have an entire country of people who love you."

"Who revere me because of my bloodline. And maybe even love the idea of me. But no person who has ever known me has ever loved me. And, as I said, no one had ever spoken the words to me before you did. I wasn't conscious of the absence of them until you brought them into my life. I wasn't aware that I had never spoken them until you spoke them to me. And it was confronting. Because it demanded something of me that I didn't want to give."

"What's that?" she asked, her voice faint, splintered.

"Humility. To get on my knees and confess to you that I needed those words. That I had been missing them my entire life. Everything in me cried out for a kind of connection that I was always denied. That I needed love. That I needed someone to be close to me. That I was desperately aching for someone to get past all of that arrogance, to love me through it, to want me no matter what. Admitting that—"

"Raphael," she said, closing the space between them and wrapping her arms around him. "I love you. But more than that, I choose you."

His big body heaved, a broken sob escaping his lips. "I love you," he said, the words untested, unfamiliar and beautiful on his lips.

She clung to him. So tight she never wanted to let go. Not because she was afraid he'd disappear, but because they'd spent far too much time not holding each other at all. "I am so honored to be the first person to hear those words from you," she whispered.

"And you won't be the last. I will say them to our son. I will say them every day. I will withhold no good thing from my child. Not now that I've allowed myself to see what really matters. What really lasts. You're right. Everything I've ever put stock in my entire life has been vanity. So easily burned away by the things of the world. But this, this is real. It's deep. It's something that can never be taken away from me. Never be taken away from you. And I... I am so grateful. Because you have given me the one thing on earth that I could never buy. That I could never force someone to give to me simply because of my title. And I think that's why it terrified me so. I knew it was something I had no power within myself to acquire. I knew it was something you would have to choose to give me. Something I could never manipulate out of you. It's why I got so angry every time you asked for me to feel something authentic. To do something other than to simply wave my hand and commit an empty gesture. You asked for real things. For deep things. I knew that in order to achieve that, I would have to allow myself to feel something real."

"I know it hurts," she said, the words choked. "I know it does. I know what it's like to let your hopes shrink smaller and smaller, so that you aim for something you can manage at least, something that you might be able to have. Something that doesn't seem too spectacular."

"I never knew to dream," he said, his voice rough. "I was given all of this and told I had the world. How could I begin to disagree?"

Her chest tightened, and she looked up into his eyes. Haunted. Wounded. That arrogance was gone for now. She felt like she should look away so that she didn't... embarrass him. So that she didn't see him like this. So raw and exposed in a way he never had been before.

She saw it all for what it was now.

His protection. Not just from the world but from the truth that lurked inside him. The fear that he, of all people, may forever want something that he wouldn't be able to have. That his birthright didn't ensure for him.

"I thought..." he began. "I thought that I didn't know need. I thought that I had never needed anything in all my life. But it turns out I am a creature made entirely from need. Who has spent all of his life covering deficiency with a host of things. With possessions and powers, as I told myself that needing was the same as devotion. That deference and worship would somehow fill a hole in my heart." He brushed his thumb over her cheek. "I didn't need. And I didn't dream. Until I met you, Bailey."

He closed his eyes for a moment, and when he opened them again they were bright. "I was furious. Furious that you could show me something about myself I had never before seen."

"A lowly waitress," she said, her tone dry.

"Do not ever say that." He shook his head, his tone fierce. "You made a prince bow down to you—how could you ever be lowly?"

"I like that your standard of greatness relates back to you."

"Naturally."

She smiled then. "I'm pleased to see your arrogance hasn't been destroyed. Only reduced."

"I am still me."

"Yes," she said. "And a good thing, too, because you're the one that I love."

And then he did the impossible one more time and got to his knees in front of her. "I want you to be my wife," he said.

"I already am." Her throat was tight, emotion building in her chest until it was impossible to breathe.

"But this time I am not demanding. This time I'm asking. This time, it is with the understanding that I am not a great gift. Not with my title and my palace. You are the gift, Bailey. You. You have changed me, changed my world."

"After I broke it," she said, a little sob breaking the words.

"It was always going to break. You uncovered the void in me—you didn't create it. And you were the only one who could ever fill it. You're my only dream."

A tear slipped down Bailey's cheek, and she knelt down with Raphael, bringing herself to the ground with him. She bracketed his cheeks with her hands, her heart so full she thought it would burst.

"I never thought a girl like me would dream of a fairy tale. But here you are, my very own Prince Charming. And do you know what the very best thing is?"

"What?" he asked, his voice rough.

She pressed her lips to his as tears slipped down her cheeks. "We're going to live happily ever after."

EPILOGUE

SANTA FIRENZE REJOICED the day their prince and his princess gave birth to their first son. Raphael felt that he got much more credit for it than he deserved, and he was the first to tell everyone so.

If anyone was surprised by the prince's sudden show of humility, they didn't say. Especially as it ran only so deep.

He was still Prince Raphael DeSantis, after all.

When he and Bailey brought their son home, he didn't allow the residents of the palace to bow to him. Instead, they had a party in the newest DeSantis's honor. They had cake of every variety, cake that Bailey heartily approved of since, as she told him, she was completely secure in her husband's heart now.

There was laughter and music, happiness that was perhaps not fitting of a man who would one day join the statues out in the courtyard, but he didn't care. Love was more important than tradition.

The oldest members of staff held the little prince, kissed his forehead. Showed him affection in a way that Raphael had never been allowed to receive.

The sight made him feel like just maybe he would do

right for this child. That just maybe he would be able to care for him in the right ways.

Much later, when he was in the bedroom with Bailey, and she was holding their son close, feeding him at her breast, he was struck with a sudden swift surge of emotion so deep, so intense that he had to go down to the floor so he didn't fall forward.

And that was how the prince, who had been bowed down to from the moment of his birth, and all throughout his life, came to kneel before a waitress. Brought down to his knees by love.

* * * * *

Don't miss the first part of Maisey Yates's
HEIRS BEFORE VOWS *trilogy*
THE SPANIARD'S PREGNANT BRIDE
Available now!

And the trilogy concludes with
THE ITALIAN'S PREGNANT VIRGIN
Available January 2017

MILLS & BOON®

MODERN™

POWER, PASSION AND IRRESISTIBLE TEMPTATION

A sneak peek at next month's titles...

In stores from 15th December 2016:

- **A Deal for the Di Sione Ring** – Jennifer Hayward
- **A Dangerous Taste of Passion** – Anne Mather
- **Married for the Greek's Convenience** – Michelle Smart
- **A Child Claimed by Gold** – Rachael Thomas

In stores from 29th December 2016:

- **The Italian's Pregnant Virgin** – Maisey Yates
- **Bought to Carry His Heir** – Jane Porter
- **Bound by His Desert Diamond** – Andie Brock
- **Defying Her Billionaire Protector** – Angela Bissell

MILLS & BOON®

EXCLUSIVE EXTRACT

Hotel magnate Nate Brunswick's faith in marriage
has been destroyed by his father – but searching
for his beloved grandfather's lost ring leads the
illegitimate Di Sione to an inconvenient engagement!
Mina Mastrantino can only pass the ring on once
she's married. A divorce should be easy…
but their exquisite wedding night gives them
both far more than they planned!

Read on for a sneak preview of
A DEAL FOR THE DI SIONE RING
by Jennifer Hayward

"You're an honorable man, Nate Brunswick. *Grazie.*"

"Not so honorable, Mina." A dark glitter entered his
eyes. "You called me improper not so long ago. I can
be that and more. I am a hard, ruthless businessman who
does what it takes to make money. I will turn a hotel
over in the flash of an eye if I don't see the flesh on the
bones I envisioned when I bought it. I will enjoy a
woman one night and send her packing the next when
I get bored of her company. Know what you're getting
into with me if you accept this. You will learn the
dog-eat-dog approach to life, *not* the civilized one."

Why did something that was intended to be a warning
send a curious shudder through her? Mina drew the wrap
closer around her shoulders, her gaze tangling with
Nate's. The glitter in his eyes stoked to a hot, velvet

shimmer as he took a step forward and ran a finger along the line of her jaw. "Rule number one of this new arrangement, should you so choose to accept it, is to not look at me like that, *wife*. If we do this, we keep things strictly business so both of us walk away after the year with exactly what we want."

Her gaze fell away from his, her blood hot and thick in her veins. "You're misinterpreting me."

"No, I'm not." He brought his mouth to her ear, his warm breath caressing her cheek. "I have a hell of a lot more experience than you do, Mina. I can recognize the signs. They were loud and clear in my hotel room that day and they're loud and clear now."

She took a deep, shuddering breath. To protest further would be futile when her skin felt like it was on fire, her knees like jelly. He watched her like a cat played with a mouse, all powerful and utterly sure of himself. "The only thing that would be more of a disaster than this day's already been," he drawled finally, apparently ready to have mercy on her, "would be for us to end up in bed together. So a partnership it is, Mina." He lifted his glass. "What do you say?"

MILLS & BOON®

Why shop at millsandboon.co.uk?

Each year, thousands of romance readers find their
perfect read at mills   se
we're passionate a   st
romantic fiction. He   es
   of shopping at

* **Get new books fi**   r
  favourite books on
  the shops

* **Get exclusive disc**   buy
  our specially create
  to 50% off the RRP

* **Find your favourite**
  interviews and new
  authors and series
  what to try next

* **Join in**—once you'v
  don't forget to register with us to rate, review and
  join in the discussions

Visit **www.millsandboon.co.uk**
for all this and more today!